Centaur Rising

Centaur Rising

JANE YOLEN

Christy Ottaviano Books
Henry Holt and Company
New York

Henry Holt and Company, LLC
Publishers since 1866
175 Fifth Avenue
New York, New York 10010
mackids.com

Henry Holt® is a registered trademark of Henry Holt and Company, LLC.
Copyright © 2014 by Jane Yolen
All rights reserved.

Library of Congress Cataloging-in-Publication Data
Yolen, Jane.
Centaur rising / Jane Yolen. — First edition.
    pages   cm
Summary: In 1965, a year after Arianne thinks she sees a shooting star land
in the fields surrounding her family's horse farm, a baby centaur is born and
the family, already under scrutiny because Arianne's six-year-old brother
has birth defects, struggles to keep the colt a secret.
ISBN 978-0-8050-9664-4 (hardback) — ISBN 978-0-8050-9665-1 (e-book)
[1. Centaurs—Fiction. 2. Horses—Fiction. 3. Farm life—Connecticut—
Fiction. 4. Abnormalities, Human—Fiction. 5. Secrets—Fiction.
6. Single-parent families—Fiction. 7. Quakers—Fiction.
8. Connecticut—History—20th century—Fiction.] I. Title.
PZ7.Y78Cen 2014
[Fic]—dc23
2014015964

Henry Holt books may be purchased for business or promotional use. For information
on bulk purchases, please contact Macmillan Corporate and Premium Sales
Department at (800) 221-7945 x5442 or by e-mail at specialmarkets@macmillan.com.

First Edition—2014 / Designed by Ashley Halsey
Printed in the United States of America by R. R. Donnelley & Sons Company,
Harrisonburg, Virginia

1 3 5 7 9 10 8 6 4 2

For the twins—Amelia and Caroline Stemple—
who simply love books.

☆ ☆ ☆

With thanks to Nora Bartlett, who told me some wonder-ful stories about a horse barn at night, and Ann Morrison, who took me out for a morning amongst the Fife Disabled young riders. With special hand waves to my extraordinary beta reader Debby Harris, my equally extraordinary editor, Christy Ottaviano, and my two cheerleaders—my amazing agent Elizabeth Harding and my daughter Heidi E. Y. Stemple, who sometimes takes extraordinary measures to either keep up with me or keep me in line.

There is something about the outside of a horse that's good for the insides of all kids, whatever their ableness.

—*Motto of the Kai's Kids Riding Academy*

AUGUST 1964

A Shower of Stars

IN THE MIDDLE OF THE NIGHT, Mom and I got out of bed, picked up Robbie from his room, put sweaters on over our pajamas, and grabbed a horse blanket from the barn. As soon as we were ready, we went out into the paddock to watch the Perseid meteor showers and count the shooting stars.

I spread out the blanket on the grass under a copse of maples so we blocked out any excess light but had a full view of the rest of the sky. Then the three of us lay down on our backs to watch.

There were occasional white sparks as stars shot across the sky. I clapped at the first one, and the second. Robbie did, too, in his own way. When the real fireworks began, we were all too awed to clap anymore. I just kept grinning, having an absolute gas.

Beside me, Robbie giggled and said, "See, Ari, like giant fireflies sailing across a bowl of milk." He talks like that a lot, when he isn't making up songs.

I've always been drawn to magic. Fairy tales, fantasy stories, worlds like Narnia and Middle Earth. Even before I could read on my own, Dad read them to me. He had this low, whispery, confiding voice that could suddenly boom out when the beast or troll or dragon appeared. No one else read me stories that way, like we were right there in the middle of the action.

I still had a musical jewelry box he'd given me after returning from one of his long tours with the band. It had a porcelain princess on top that turned around and around as "Somewhere Over the Rainbow" played. Mom made the princess wings out of pipe cleaners and lace so that she looked like a fairy. I called her Fairy Gwendoline. The song was tinkly and off-key, but it became my definition of magic. Or at least storybook magic, looking good and creaking along with a clockwork heart. As for real magic, I didn't know any.

Maybe it all left with Dad.

Lying on the blanket, I thought about wishing on a star or on the Perseids. But they were just gigantic balls of light. High magic is not about science and star showers. I tore this quote out of a magazine and posted it above my mirror so I could read it every day: "Magic is about the unpredictable, the stunningly original, the not-containable or attainable. It can't be guessed at or imitated or asked for. It happens and then it's gone."

And no, I wasn't thinking about my dad.

At that point, our old pony Agora came over, looking at us as if puzzled that her humans were lying on the grass in the middle of the night. Easing to the ground on her arthritic knees, she snuggled up to us, whickering softly. Horses have a common magic, and they never let you down.

"She's more puppy than pony," Mom said, which made me laugh. It was good to laugh with her. That didn't happen often anymore. I suddenly realized how much I missed it.

We were having a difficult time in our lives. That's what Martha, our barn manager, called it. She was like a second mom to me. Six years before, when I was seven, and two weeks after Robbie had been born, Dad had left without an explanation. He'd never called or sent a letter afterwards. The bank mailed my mom a check from him every month that barely covered the farm's mortgage. A really small check, considering what a famous rock star he is. Not Elvis famous. Not Bill Haley famous. Not Bobby Darin famous. But famous enough. We didn't even know where he was most times, except when his band's name appeared in the paper playing somewhere very far away, like San Diego or England.

I was still upset over his leaving, but Mom didn't seem to be. Right after he left, she'd said, "He wasn't actually here when he was *here*, you know," which I hadn't understood at the time.

After that, Mom and I never talked about much of anything

except horses, my chores, and school. Since I could read on my own and got good grades, did my barn chores on time and without complaint, our conversations became fewer and fewer.

I didn't have many friends. I first began to understand my lack of friends when earlier in the year some nutty guy on the news preached that the world was going to end before fall. Mom had laughed when she heard it, a sound as creaky and off-key as my old fairy princess box had been. "I thought six years of endings was enough," she said, which was the closest she'd ever come to having the Dad Conversation with me. Besides, we didn't believe in world's end stuff. We were Quakers, which meant we believed that doing good, and peace work, in this life was important. We believed that each of us had God inside of us, and we had to listen to that still, small voice of love and reason, not some bearded guy in Heaven who was going to make the world end.

The kids in school talked about the prophecy, and some of them were scared. I thought it was silly to be scared of something like that and said out loud that only idiots believed such things. Jake Galla called me a Communist for saying that, which made no sense at all, and I told him so in front of our history class. A couple of the kids laughed, and Brain Brian even applauded.

I ignored Jake, having been called worse: Horse, Nitwit, and Ari-Fairy being the most common. It's not exactly true that words can never harm you, but as long as you can learn to shrug them off, you can get along okay. I'd learned from the best— Martha.

Instead, I sometimes talked in front of the lockers with a few of the kids about our principal's latest hair color, or what "Whole Lotta Shakin' Goin' On" really meant. You'd never guess what Brain Brian thought it means! But talking to a few kids a few times in school didn't translate into friendships. And besides, I had a lot of chores to do at the farm.

However, that August night, lying on the blanket with Robbie and Mom, looking at the star-streaked sky, it seemed the world was more like a light show than lights-out, more mechanics than magic, and even if I never got to share the Perseids with a best friend, I had Mom and Robbie and Agora, and I was okay with that.

Suddenly a huge star flashed right over the Suss farm next door, where the Morgan mares had been turned out into their field. I sat up, leaning on my left elbow as the mares startled, snorted wildly, and kicked up their heels.

Half awake, Robbie murmured, "Far out! And far away, too!"

At that exact moment, Agora got up a bit shakily, shook her head—which made her long mane dance about—and trotted over to the fence as if wanting to get closer to the show.

"Time for bed," Mom said, standing. She grabbed up Robbie, balanced him on her hip, and headed for the house.

I didn't complain. Chores start early on a farm, and I'm grumpy without at least a full eight hours of sleep. Even if it's broken up. So, I just folded the blanket and started after them.

As we went through the paddock gate, I heard a strange whinny, like a waterfall of sound. Looking back, I saw something white and glowing sail over the fence between the Suss farm and ours, that high double fence that no horse—not even a champion jumper—can get across.

At first I thought it was a shooting star. Then I thought it was more likely ball lightning. And for a moment, I wondered if it might be the actual end of the world, in case we Quakers were wrong. Even as I had that thought and suspected I was dreaming, I took off after Mom and Robbie at a run, vowing to write about it in my journal in the morning.

JULY 1965

Agora's Surprise

A MARE IS PREGNANT between 320 and 370 days, about a full year. Ponies give birth a bit earlier, more like eleven months. Mom taught me about that when we first came to the farm as renters, long before we bought out the old owner with the money she got from the divorce. When we moved here to Massachusetts, I was three, Mom and Dad were married, and Robbie wasn't even a blip on the horizon, as Mom likes to say.

Mom grew up in Connecticut with horses and knows *everything* about them, even though her old farm, Long Riders, is long gone. As are my grandparents. A cul-de-sac of new houses sits on the old ménage and pasture, and the old farmhouse has become a gas station and general store. We drove past it once. It made Mom sad. Still, she knows horses inside and out, and what she doesn't know, Martha does.

If Mom's the owner of our farm, Martha McKean is its heart. Our riders call her "a regular horse whisperer," and sometimes "the Queen"—except Mrs. Angotti, who once called Martha "Ivan the Terrible," and the name stuck. Mom explained to me that Ivan was some Russian king nobody liked and who was really awful to everybody. Now everyone says it as a joke, and even Martha smiles at it.

Martha's not awful at all, she just doesn't like people much. Except she tolerates Mom and bosses Robbie and me around something fierce. Martha prefers horses, and it's easy to guess why. The horses listen to her, and they do what she tells them to, almost as if she's their lead mare. The rest of us listen when we want to, which isn't often enough to please Martha.

So, near Thanksgiving last year, when Martha came into our house at dinnertime, a green rubber band in her hair, and said to Mom, "Old Aggie's got something in her belly," we listened, horrified.

Martha's the only one to call Agora "Old Aggie." I once asked her why, and she shrugged, saying, "Aggie told me to," like it was no big deal that horses talked to her.

Mom's hands went up to her mouth. She looked over at

me, green eyes shining strangely, like a cat about to cry. Then the little pinch lines between her eyes showed up as she struggled to control herself, and I knew that there'd be no tears. There never are.

"Colitis?" I whispered to Martha.

It was the worst thing I could think of. If colitis hits a horse's belly, it usually dies within hours, a day at most. We've never lost a horse to colitis, or anything else.

Martha warns us about once a month that losing a horse is bound to happen someday and we'd best be prepared. Times she talks like that, Mom calls her Aunty Dark Cloud.

Strangely, Martha laughed, a high whinnying sound. "Nah, not colitis. That old pony's up and got herself pregnant."

"Can't have," I said. "She'd need a stallion for—"

"Must be three months gone." Martha's hand described a small arc over her own belly.

Counting back on my fingers, I got to August, the month of the shooting stars.

Mom must have done the same counting. She said, "That darn Jove. I'll call over and . . ."

Jove, the big Suss stud, had gotten out more times than we could count. It's why we finally had to build the double-rowed fence between our fields and the Suss farm. We couldn't really afford it, and Mom had called it "the most expensive birth deterrent ever," but if we left it to Mr. Suss, it wasn't going to happen.

Robbie laughed. "Aggie's gonna have a baby!" he said. "Will it be bigger than her if Jove is the dad?"

Martha ignored him, shook her head, and said to Mom, "Old man Suss would have been over here yammering away at you had that rascal Jove got loose again. Suss would already be charging you a stud fee, like he's done before. But he's said nary a word, Miz Martins." She never called Mom by her first name.

"Then how . . . ?"

It was the one question that troubled us the entire year of Agora's pregnancy. But eventually I thought the two of them were looking in the wrong place for answers. I knew this was true magic in our lives at last, and the answer was in the sky.

☆ ☆ ☆

I've never seen Martha out of uniform: those rumpled and stained blue jeans, a white or gray T-shirt in the summer and, in the winter, a dark-blue sweater with a hole in one sleeve. She wears sneakers in sun, rain, or snow, not like

Mom who's almost always in jodhpurs and boots with a well-ironed shirt during the day and a long Indian print dress in the evening after barn chores are done.

Martha's gray hair is usually tied back in a ponytail with a fat colored rubber band, red when she's feeling good, green when worried, blue when it's best to leave her alone. Mom's hair is pulled back in an ashy blond French braid when she rides, though at night it sits like a cloud on her shoulders. Is she beautiful? Dad used to say so. He called her the princess of ice and snow. He was dark to her light, heat to her ice. Or so Martha said once, and I never forgot it.

Sometimes I think Martha is probably part horse herself. And that's what my English teacher calls a GOM, a good old-fashioned metaphor. Of course she's truly human through and through, something I came to understand during the year after that night in the pasture when the stars fell all around us and a ball of lightning leaped over the fence.

☆ ☆ ☆

Mom and Robbie and I live in the big farmhouse. It has fifteen rooms. "Far too many for just us," Mom says whenever we have an all-family cleaning day. We can't afford help, except for Martha, who only does the barn work. So Mom and I do the mopping and dusting while Robbie in his wheelchair is piled high with cleaning stuff that he hands out as we make our way around the house.

Maybe the house *is* too big for us, though I remember when Dad was here, how he seemed to fill the place up with all his stuff. In those days, we had a guitar room, a pool table room, plus a band room attached to two recording rooms that Dad called The Studio. And then there were bedrooms for all his band mates and roadies to stay over in as well. These days we just have empty rooms and loads of doors in the hallway that we keep closed year-round.

The old band room on the first floor is now Robbie's bedroom, with its specially made shower that a friend of Mom's built in one of the old recording rooms, trading his work so that his kids could have a year of free riding.

When Robbie was born, Dad left and took with him all the people who'd moved in—including the special nurse who was supposed to help care for Robbie but instead became a special backup singer in his band. We never got another nurse, because Mom just didn't have the money for one. She moved her bed into the old pool table room so she could be right next door to Robbie. That left me with the entire upstairs. So I have a playroom and a music room and a room for my riding trophies. And there's two extra rooms for friends, if I ever have any friends who want to stay over.

We even have room for Martha to live with us, but she has a one-bedroom cottage on the other side of our driveway. She'd been living there when we arrived, and she likes her privacy. In fact, she likes it so much, I've never been invited inside. But I bet it has horse pictures on the walls.

✯ ✯ ✯

Agora's pregnancy seemed routine, which was good. Because of her arthritis and her age, we'd always figured giving birth would be too hard on her, so we'd never had her bred. But then she accidentally bred herself.

Nevertheless, we were all really concerned. Agora had been a rescue pony whose last owner had nearly starved her to death. Martha said the owner should have been put in jail for life! I'm sure she was just making a joke. Well, *almost* sure.

Dr. Herks, the vet, checked her out once a month during her pregnancy, until the last two months, and then he came to see her every other week. Martha grumbled that he was around the farm so much, he was like a puppy underfoot.

Mom just laughed at Martha. "It's nice to have a vet so dedicated to his work," she said. "And since this is Agora's first foal . . ."

"And last," Martha reminded us.

☆ ☆ ☆

The day everything changed on the farm was the day Agora went into labor. It was Saturday morning, and I was doing the usual barn chores, mucking out stalls, putting in fresh straw, filling water buckets. I'd just finished the stalls of the old men, as we called our aging geldings.

Robbie was with me, sitting in his wheelchair, telling me bad six-year-old jokes. I mean the jokes six-year-olds tell, not that the jokes were six years old. He gets them from books and from our small black-and-white television set. I didn't have time to watch much TV, what with my homework and barn chores, so Robbie used to catch me up on everything he'd seen—mainly *Bewitched*, *Flipper*, *The*

Munsters, *Daniel Boone*, *Mister Ed*, and *The Addams Family*. He would have watched all day if Mom had let him. And he could go on and on about the shows to anyone who'd listen. Half the time, I didn't pay any attention, just nodded and did my homework or my chores. I didn't let him know I wasn't completely involved in every plot turn and joke, or he'd never stop explaining.

Martha talked that way, too, on and on, with me tuning out. All she did was tell me how to do what I'd been doing for the past four years, since I was nine. Calling me "Little Bit" and "Shortie," even though I was neither of those anymore. Calling Robbie "Squinch" (because of his glasses) and "Munchkin" (because he's so small).

Martha wanted things done right, meaning her way, so how could I be mad at her? Annoyed a little, irritated some, but not mad. Martha was an itch we all had to scratch.

And Robbie? He just called her silly names back: "Marmar" when he was little, "Mairzy Doats" from a song Martha used to sing, and now "Marmalade" from his favorite jam, which is so bitter, I won't eat it. "More for me," he always says.

★ ★ ★

I rolled Robbie to Agora's stall next, and we could hear rough breathing. When I peeked in, Agora was standing with her head hanging down, and she didn't look good.

"Keep an eye on her, buddy," I said to Robbie, "I've got to call the vet."

"Will she be okay?" I could hear the tightness in his voice.

"Dr. Herks is the best," I reminded him. "Try and keep her calm."

He nodded. "I'll sing to her." He loved singing to the horses. He had a great voice, always right on key. Not like me. Mom says it's the one good thing he got from Dad.

I left Robbie at the open door, not that there was much he could do if things went wrong. He can't use his legs, his pelvic bones are missing, his arms are too short, and his hands are like flippers because the fingers and thumbs grew fused together.

But that voice . . . Martha calls it angelic, only not to his face. He was already singing to Agora, to keep her calm. "A horse is a horse, of course, of course. . . ." It was the theme song from *Mister Ed*.

★ ★ ★

I'd seen mares in labor before. Their tails twitch high, and sometimes they stomp about the stall as if they can't quite settle. Then, suddenly, they collapse on the ground, rolling over on one side, the water flooding out of their hind ends. Several long pushes later, a white sac like a balloon comes out with one or two tiny horse hooves showing.

The first time I watched a mare have a baby, I thought it was disgusting. Yet once the foal stood up, shaking all over and then walking about on its spindly legs, everything was so magical, I forgot about the icky stuff.

But what I was hearing that day from Agora's stall didn't sound like magic. It sounded like pain. I couldn't take time to comfort her. Robbie would have to do that. He was good with the horses since, unlike most kids his age, he didn't make quick movements or too much noise.

I ran to the barn phone.

The vet's number was written on the wall over the phone in black paint. As Martha said, "Pieces of paper can get torn off or lost, but black paint is forever."

He answered on the first ring, his voice low, musical. "Gerry Herks here." He always sounded like a movie star,

though he didn't actually look like one. Just pleasant-faced
with brown eyes and graying hair.

"Arianne Martins here."

"Everything all right at the farm?"

"It's Agora. It's . . ."

"It's time," he said brightly. "I'll be right there."

2

The Vet Vet

MOM ONCE TOLD ME that the word *pony* was originally French. Or a word sort of like it: *poulenet*. The French didn't actually mean a pony like Agora, who, even fully grown, is only the size of a small horse. *Poulenet* means a baby horse, a foal.

Agora is a white pony. Yet if you brush your hand over the top layer of her back, underneath the white hair is a gray coat. You might call that magical, but it's real.

Her mane is thick, and so is her tail. When I asked Mom why, she shrugged, saying, "It's characteristic of ponies." Then she'd turned back to sorting grain sales brochures.

Agora's mane is thicker than the manes of our four other mares—Hera, Helen, Hester, and Hope. (Mom has an *H* fetish, since her own name is Hannah.) Thicker than the manes of our two geldings—Aragorn and Boromir. (I was reading *The Lord of the Rings* when we named them.) Now we just call them Gorn and Bor.

In fact, Agora's mane is much thicker than any of the manes of our nine boarding horses as well. As much mystery as magic.

From the beginning, one of my special chores has been brushing and braiding Agora's mane. Each time I come near her with the brush, she sidles close, rubs up against my hip, then nuzzles my palm, and we begin.

☆ ☆ ☆

Once I knew that Dr. Herks was on his way, I ran back to Agora's stall, not even taking time to call Mom out. I knew she was working on the barn bills and hated being disturbed when it was the bill-paying time of the month.

Besides, Dr. Herks had said that since Agora was old, things should move slowly. Especially as this was her first pregnancy. So I figured I had plenty of time to get Mom once the vet arrived. From the way he sounded on the phone, I guessed he was hurrying, and he was only fifteen minutes away.

Agora was already lying down, and Martha—a blue rubber band in her hair—was sitting in the straw by her side. Agora's head was in Martha's lap, and the two of them looked as if they were having a friendly talk, though Agora's belly was bouncing in an alarming way.

Martha must have nudged Robbie's chair to one side in her rush to get in, because it was smack up against the near wall and turned sideways. That made it hard for him to see what was going on. And with his shortened arms, he had trouble enough working the wheels on a flat, paved walk. There was no way he could do anything in the stall.

I pushed him around so he could watch. "Dr. Herks is on his way."

"I told her," Robbie said.

Martha never looked up.

"He sounded a bit . . ." I thought a minute before saying it. "A bit nervous."

"He should be." Martha was still looking down at Agora, her voice quiet, soothing. She was brushing her fingers through Agora's mane.

"*I'm* not nervous," Robbie said. "*I'm* excited!" This would be the first time he'd been allowed to watch a birth.

"It can be pretty scuzzy," I warned.

"Scuzzy is my second name!"

"Your *second* name is Connor," I said, "Robert Connor Martins. But if you get sick, don't expect anyone to help you. We'll be too busy." I turned to Martha. "Anything more I can do?"

She looked at me as if sizing me up, and finding me ready for the task, said, "Boil water."

"Really?"

She snorted, a very horsy sound. "An old joke."

"Joke?"

"Doctors used to have expectant dads boil water just to keep them busy and out of the way. I bet your dad did that when you were born."

"I wouldn't know," I said, "since I was a baby then!" I didn't want to visit that particular hurt. "I think he was on the road with his band anyway."

"Don't snap at me, Missy. You're still a youngster to me, for all you're grown up in so many ways."

It was pure Martha, of course. She can never just apologize. But I got the hint and went to clean out the rest of the stalls, leaving Robbie behind.

☆ ☆ ☆

The horses knew something was up. Hope—who'd never done anything of the sort—was so anxious, she accidentally slammed a hoof down on my right foot not once, but twice, and boy, did *that* hurt.

Gorn, normally the sweetest of the horses, tried to get out the door, shouldering me aside so roughly, I had to haul him back by his mane.

Just then I heard a rumbly Jeep drive up and knew it had to be Dr. Herks, so I went out to greet him.

Dr. Herks has a face that's handsome enough in some lights, but there are wrinkle lines on his forehead that look like the stripes on a flag, and deep grooves around his eyes. He's about six feet tall and all muscle, which helps when you're pushing big animals around. But he doesn't act tough, which was something Dad, who was only about five foot nine, always did. When I think about him—and it's not that often—it's always him yelling at his band members and roadies and cursing. I've never heard anyone else cursing like that. Mom flinches if I even say "drat!" or "darn!"

By contrast, Dr. Herks is a softie. You can hear it in his voice when he talks to the horses, but he still manages to keep them in their places. Martha admires that and says so often. Never to his face, of course. In fact, she bosses him around as if he was a kid.

Sometimes I had the feeling that Dr. Herks had a crush on Mom, and I kind of hoped she liked him back. I bet he'd make a great dad. And yeah, it would help with our vet bills, too. And then he wouldn't have to stay in the apartment over his operating room, which Martha called "living over the store" and was an odd thing to say, since that's sort of what we do, too. Except we aren't *over* it, but on the side.

"How's it going?" Dr. Herks asked as he got out of the car.

"I'm supposed to be boiling water."

He smiled. "Good. I'm going to need all the help that I can get."

"I thought that was supposed to be a joke."

"The help part is no joke." He winked.

I nodded. "I'll give you all I've got. But I think we'd better hurry."

"Hurrying here," he said as he grabbed his doctor bag and headed toward the barn.

I matched him step for step, which wasn't easy because he had really long legs. It meant I had to run.

At the barn, I swung open the door to Agora's stall to let Dr. Herks go through.

"About time, Herkel," Martha said in her no-nonsense voice.

"Gosh . . ." I could barely breathe.

Dr. Herks had put down his black bag and was pulling on a pair of rubber gloves without looking at either Martha or Agora.

But I'd looked.

Agora was panting heavily, still over on her side, but she'd already given birth. Martha was holding the brand-new foal, unsteady on its feet and still wet from its birthing.

A foal.

Or something. It was hard to say if I was dreaming or the light was bad. It was . . . nothing I'd ever seen before.

A cold shudder ran through me. Maybe fear, maybe disgust. It sure wasn't wonder or awe.

"Isn't that the coolest thing you've ever seen?" Robbie asked. "Not gross at all."

"Gosh," I said again, because the foal was only a pony from its hooves to the top of its body. Where it should have had horse shoulders, where the pony neck and head should have been, it looked just like a baby boy, with arms and hands, curly reddish hair, blue eyes, and a big toothless grin.

"Gosh!" I said a third time. For someone who desperately wanted magic in her life, that was a pretty small response. But as Martha often said, wanting and getting can be difficult neighbors. And from all the fantasy books I'd read, I knew that the line between gargoyle and angel could be pretty thin.

The pony boy was too new and too strange for me to really take in. I wasn't thinking magic, I was thinking *mistake.*

Dr. Herks finally looked over at Martha. His eyes widened.

"Centaur," said Martha, "I never . . ."

"No one never," said Dr. Herks, which was totally ungrammatical but made perfect sense. And then he fainted, which didn't make any sense at all. Crumpling down from such a height, it was amazing that he didn't smash his head on the wall.

Now, that was something I *really* didn't understand. I mean, Dr. Herks wasn't just a vet, but a Vet—a marine who'd fought in Vietnam and been decorated for bravery. And wounded, too, Mom had said. Wounded, but not badly. Just badly enough.

"Get your mother," ordered Martha. "I've got my hands too full with this pony boy here, Agora there, and Robbie by the wall, to be able to manage a fainting vet." She seemed unimpressed—or at least undisturbed—by the magic or whatever it was in front of her, just as if creatures out of myth had always been born in our barn.

"You don't have to manage me, Mrs. Grump," said Robbie.

"I do when you need managing, Munchkin!"

I was happy to be out of there, but Mom must have seen Dr. Herks' Jeep in the driveway, because she was already standing in the doorway of the stall, and I nearly ran right into her.

"Good grief," she said, then added, "Gerry?" in a strange voice, and went to kneel by his side, which may have been the strangest thing of all.

3

Pony Boy

So THERE WE WERE, Agora on *her* side, Dr. Herks on *his* side, and Mom with her arms around him. Martha was holding the newborn whatever. Robbie looked astonishingly pleased, but me, I was just agog.

Agog was Martha's word, not mine. She had just said to me, "Hey, Ari-bari, stop opening your mouth like a frog, all agog, and do something."

"Boil water?"

She made an annoyed *tsk*ing sound, as if she'd never heard of any such thing.

I knew better than to ask her what I *should* do then, just as Agora got to her feet. She went right to her foal, pushing Martha aside, and started nuzzling him clean, making no distinction between the horse part and the boy part. He was simply hers all over.

All at once, I knew she was right. *Maybe*, I thought, *I should forget fear and concentrate on awe.* At least I hadn't passed out.

It was a start.

Meanwhile, Agora was simply doing what a mare does with a new foal. When she got to his face, he giggled and pushed her away, then giggled again before struggling out between her front legs. He was wobbly—who wouldn't be with those four legs each trying to go in a different direction?—and waved his little hands about for balance. Wrinkling his nose at all the new smells, he took a couple of tentative baby steps, and then headed straight for Robbie, who was the only one his size.

Robbie held out his foreshortened arms. The pony boy stuck his head between them and nuzzled Robbie's face. They stayed that way for about a minute, and then the pony boy turned a bit unsteadily and found his way back to Agora, where he began to nurse, his tiny hands kneading her sides. The curls on his head, like wriggly red worms, were already dry, and they bounced as he drank the milk.

Now that I'd gotten over the strangeness, a part of me was suddenly jealous. After all, I was the only one who'd wanted magic in my life, and the magic had just gone over to Robbie instead. But Robbie needed the magic more than I did, so I fought the jealous thought down and smiled. It was a crooked smile, but I let it stay pasted on my face.

"Well!" Martha said. "What was *that* all about?"

"We're brothers," Robbie announced. "We even look alike."

"Don't be dumb," I said, smile disappearing faster than a Cheshire cat's. "He's a . . . a horse. And you . . . well, you aren't."

"But I'm half something, just like he is. Half *seal*, the kids said at my old school."

"Those kids were stupid, mean," I said, "and plain ignorant."

"Ignorant *is* stupid," Robbie said.

"Not all the time," I told him. "You aren't ignorant, not by a long shot. But saying you and the pony boy look alike is stupid. You don't look anything like him." I took a deep breath. "He's got red curly hair and bright blue eyes. You're like me. Auburn hair, slate blue eyes, and . . ." I didn't say we both looked like Dad, not Mom. I knew that, but how could Robbie have known? We had no photos of Dad around.

"A *seal*?" Martha said flatly. "Whatever gave them that silly idea?"

I knew but didn't say it aloud. Robbie was a thalidomide kid, and the newspapers had dubbed all thalidomide kids "seal children" because many of them had flipper arms and sometimes flipper legs. Robbie's arms ended at the elbow, where there were only two fingers and a thumb.

None of it was his fault, of course. It was just the result of pills Mom had been given when she was first pregnant with him. Mom hadn't just had morning sickness; she'd thrown up all day long, hour after hour, till she cried with the pain. Dad had gotten the thalidomide pills for her when he was on tour in Toronto and Montreal since they were supposed to be a miracle cure for pregnant women who threw up a lot. And the pills *did* cure that. But it turned out they were a kind of poison, too, destroying parts of babies before they were ever born.

"Seal children." Once that name hit the newspapers, the parents of one of the kids at school called Robbie that, and soon the kids all did, too. It was why Mom took him out of school and taught him at home.

Why she hadn't any time for me.

Why she'd hardly ever laughed these past six years.

"The pony boy *knows* me," Robbie insisted. "And I know him. We're brothers."

"You're my brother, not his," I said.

Dr. Herks had already come to and was sitting up, his eyes still a bit unfocused. Then he saw the pony boy and looked ready to pass out again.

Mom put a hand on his arm and gave me a fierce stare. "Ari, I could use help here! Dr. Herks needs some air."

So I came over to help, but by then Dr. Herks had gotten up by himself. He walked a bit unsteadily out of the stall, saying, "I'm fine, Hannah, fine. Don't fuss."

"I'm not fussing," she said, running a hand through her hair, which made it look even more like a blond cloud. "I'm being practical. We need a vet here, and you're it."

Then she turned to me. "Get your brother out of there. Agora needs time to bond with her . . . her . . . baby."

"I think she's already—" I began, but Mom was saying to Dr. Herks, "If you're going to faint again, Gerry, at least do it where you won't disturb *them*." She pointed over her shoulder back at Agora and her foal.

I suddenly remembered her saying something like that before: "If you're going to call me that, don't do it where Arianne can hear." Or maybe it was "If you're really going to leave, don't do it when Arianne's awake." Which might have been why Dad left without saying good-bye.

I pushed Robbie's wheelchair out into the walkway between the stalls, trying to avoid hitting either Mom or Dr. Herks, who was still as wobbly as a colt.

"I never . . . ," he began, embarrassed, stopped, looked down at the floor, and began again. "I've never fainted in my life, Hannah. And I've delivered some pretty startling creatures in my time."

"I'm sure you have," Mom said. She was looking where he was looking.

"Nope—never fainted."

"I meant you've delivered some strange . . ."

And then they both looked up, staring at each other, saying, "Sorry. Sorry," their voices fitting together like a song.

"What do we do now?" Dr. Herks asked. I wasn't sure if he was talking about the pony boy or about Mom.

Mom said at the same time, "We don't ignore it or turn our backs on it."

"Him!" Robbie said loudly.

Mom and Dr. Herks both looked at us as if just noticing we were there. As if just realizing they were talking about the pony boy.

"The foal is a *he*, not an it," I explained.

"I knew that," Dr. Herks said.

"Right," Mom said, a beat later. "We don't call the newspapers or *Life* magazine or *Newsweek* or *Time*, or anything like that."

I rubbed my left arm hard with my right palm. "He's just a baby."

"You got it," Dr. Herks said. "Not the AP wire or UPI or—"

"And Mrs. Angotti and the other riders and parents, none of them can know," Mom added.

They were both speaking quickly, not looking at each other, but at Robbie and me.

"We protect him," I said firmly.

"*I'll* protect him," Robbie added.

Mom and Dr. Herks stared at the two of us with identical expressions, saying together, "Agreed," though they were talking to each other, not us.

At that moment, Martha came out of the stall. "Doc, you get back in there and check that little guy out. He may need a bit more than I can give him. And no fainting this time, mister. Understand?"

He grinned. "Won't happen again, Miss Martha. One surprise is all you get."

"Didn't surprise me a bit." She looked at Mom and Robbie and me. "This has got to be a secret, you know."

"Already decided, Martha," Mom said.

"Was anyone planning to tell *me*?"

"You were busy," Mom told her.

"So were you." Martha's voice was like a whip. Mom ignored her.

We all went back to the door to watch Dr. Herks look the foal over. He checked hooves, eyes, listened to the foal's heart, temperature, mouth, tail. Then he petted and praised Agora before standing up, black bag in hand.

"Sound little guy," Dr. Herks said. "Ought to do well. Considering . . ."

"Considering what?" Martha's voice was tense.

"Considering we've no idea who his dad is or how big he's going to grow."

"Like a horse," said Martha. "We know how horses and ponies grow."

"Horses," Dr. Herks said carefully, "mature much faster than humans."

A long silence filled the stall. None of us said that horses also don't live as long as humans. We didn't have to.

In the middle of the silence, Dr. Herks turned and re-examined the pony boy with his stethoscope, then cocked his head.

"Something else?" Mom asked.

He made a face, pursed his lips, took a deep breath. "He's got two hearts."

"*Two* hearts?" Martha dismissed this with a snort.

"One in his boy chest," Dr. Herks said, "and one down in the horse chest, where it ought to be."

"What does that mean?" I asked.

"It means he's got twice as much love to give," Robbie said and opened his short arms as wide as they would go, which startled the pony boy, who giggled and hid behind Agora before turning to nurse again.

We waited breathlessly for Dr. Herks' answer.

"Darned if I know," he said, adding quickly, "Maybe Robbie's right and it's a good thing."

"See?" Robbie crowed. "I'm right!"

We chewed on what Dr. Herks had said for a while, thinking about what might happen later, when the owners came to comb and curry their horses and the kids arrived for riding lessons. When George, who delivers the feed, came by in his old pickup.

And the mailman.

And the paper girl.

Our farm's surrounded by a small town on three sides and National Forest on the fourth. Everyone knows everything that happens here. As Martha often says,

"Sneeze at this end of town, and when you reach the other end, someone's bound to say 'Gesundheit!'"

So, I thought, *what do we do about that?* But before I could say any such thing, the foal let out a strange sound, part whinny, part laugh, and I sighed quietly, thinking, *Magic! It has to be.*

Agora nuzzled him, making small contented noises. She, at least, had no questions and—I was sure—no fears about the future.

4

Settling In

"WE BETTER START BY MAKING A QUARANTINE STALL and moving the other horses to stalls in the front barn," Dr. Herks said to Mom, all business now. "Hang blankets on the bars over this stall's windows and door, so no one can see in. I'll arrange for some extra lighting so it's not too dark in here. You get out the word that the foal has . . ." He thought a minute, then shook himself like a dog after a bath. "He has *Puericentaurcephalitis*. Tell them we don't want it spreading. But that there's absolutely no danger as long as he and Agora are left alone. Oh—and also tell them you and Martha and Arianne will be in full quarantine outfits whenever attending them."

"What's that?" I asked.

"*Puericentaurcephalitis*. I just made it up. Dog Latin for boy-centaur disease. It won't fool any actual vets, or any

Latin teachers for that matter, but it'll do for now. I'll think of something better later. You know, we vets are always changing our diagnoses anyway. Should I write it down?"

"No, I meant quarantine outfits."

"Oh, *that*." He smiled. "Green jumpsuits, latex gloves, white masks over your nose and mouth."

"Can I have an outfit, too?" asked Robbie.

"Nope, because if someone sees you, and wants to help push you, how can we explain that away?" Mom said.

"He can have my outfit," Martha said. "I'm not going to dress in that. It'll scare the horses. It'll scare Old Aggie for sure."

"Mom . . ." Robbie's face was full of hope.

"Nope," she said in the way that was final.

"It will only be for show," Dr. Herks said. "Take the kit off when you're in the stall, behind the curtains. And, Robbie—you can go in the evenings, after everyone is gone. That way no one will know."

Robbie's face lit up again.

"And where do I get that . . . um . . . kit?" Mom asked, her voice softening.

"I've got plenty for when I do operations back at the clinic," he said. "I'll bring a bunch over later this morning.

As you don't actually have to be sterile, you can use them again and again. And if anyone sees me, it helps reinforce that this is an unusual situation."

"Besides," I said, "you're the only one who can say *Puericentaurwhatchmacallit*."

"Don't be a smart-hat," Martha warned me.

"I can say it!" Robbie crowed, and proceeded to prove it, not once, but several times, and then sang it to the tune of "Frere Jacques" with additional words he made up on the spot.

> *Puericentaurcephalitis,*
> *That's its name, that's its name.*
> *Can you say it with me, can you say it with me?*
> *What a shame. What a shame.*

"What a kid!" Dr. Herks said to Mom.

"Oh, he does that all the time. Mom calls it his party trick."

As for Robbie, he was too busy singing loudly and banging his hands on the arms of his wheelchair to hear what I said.

☆ ☆ ☆

After Dr. Herks left, Martha hand-lettered a sign that read QUARITINE and put it on Agora's stall. "Till we figure out what to do."

"That's not spelled right," I said.

Hands on hips, she glared at me. "People will understand."

"It still doesn't make it right." I was a champion speller in school. Won the all-school spelling bee three years in a row, which didn't help make me popular. Between the spelling and the fact that I always had to get back right after school to do my horse chores, and Mom not wanting kids over who might laugh at Robbie, I had no friends I could bring home. Most of them thought me weird anyway, so I didn't care. Well, maybe I did—a little. But not enough to do anything about it.

There were two girls from another of the middle schools who occasionally took riding lessons from Mom, Patti and Maddi. They were both a year ahead of me, but we still got to talk some. Horse talk mostly. But, since we went to different schools, we didn't hang around together except at the barn.

I went into the house, printed out the right spelling of *quarantine* with markers on a piece of yellow poster board, and brought it back to the barn.

Begrudgingly, Martha put it next to the first sign, saying, "Let 'em choose." Then she locked the stall door, stuck the key in her back pocket, and left to get Agora clean bedding straw.

Robbie was already back in the house doing his homework, so Mom and I began to move all the other horses to the near side of the barn, which shouldn't have been difficult, but they were all a bit spooked. I think they sensed the magic even if they hadn't seen it. We didn't want to move Agora and the foal. We didn't know how fragile he might be.

"And we don't want anyone seeing him by accident," Mom added.

"Who could do that?" I asked.

"The milkman or encyclopedia salesmen knocking at the door at the worst time."

"Like right when we're moving him?"

She touched her pointer finger to her nose and grinned. "Bingo!" It was something she hadn't said in a long time.

☆ ☆ ☆

We started with Hera. She's the boss of all the other horses. If we could get her to move stalls quickly and without a fuss, the rest would be easy.

"Well, *easier*," Mom said.

Hera stared at me with her deep brown eyes. She's a dainty Arabian mare with large nostrils. There was something different in her eyes that morning. Someone who didn't know her well might have said that it was a look of alarm. But really, she just looked confused.

Basically, Hera hates change. New straw, different food, a new rider—and she shows her displeasure, usually by gnawing on the side of the stall window. We have to make a new frame for that window at least once a year.

I rubbed her nose, especially where the halter strap crossed. She leaned into my hand, her nose soft and warm, while I made comforting noises. Quickly, I snapped on her lead. Then I rubbed her neck. "I know you like your own stall. But I promise, you'll like the new stall even more."

She didn't look convinced. In a horse that could mean that the whites of her eyes showed or that her ears were lying flat. Or a dozen other little things. Hera looked longingly at the window, opening her mouth and grinding her teeth, but I held the lead tightly to keep her from gnawing on the frame.

As we headed out of the stall, she whickered and the other horses answered her. But even if she wasn't convinced that everything was all right, she trusted me.

"I think we're okay," I called back in a loud whisper to Mom who was in the next stall, where Bor was stabled.

I spoke too soon.

I could see little runnels of fear, like worms under Hera's skin, skimming along her back and sides as she tried to look over her shoulder toward Agora's stall.

Without warning, she gave a loud whinny and planted all four feet on the ground, refusing to go a step farther. I tugged and tugged on the lead. It was like trying to move a mountain.

The barn erupted in whinnies and snorts and odd coughing sounds as the horses reacted to Hera's call.

Mom stuck her head out of Bor's stall and stared at me. "Not *all* right, then?"

I shrugged.

"Guess they know something's wrong."

"There's nothing *wrong*!" I said. Magic wasn't wrong. It was just . . . strange. But horses don't like strange. A lot of *people* don't like it either.

That was when I remembered the Perseids, the light and the power flowing over the fence, the mares in the Suss field startled and kicking up their heels, making this same kind of snorting fuss. Remembering the scene was like a lightbulb clicking on over my head.

"I know how it happened!" I called to Mom.

Something in my voice made Hera look up. Her eyes and ears suddenly seemed a lot more natural. So I gave her a small tug, and then a harder one, clicked my tongue against the top of my mouth, and at last she started walking again.

I led her down the corridor, out the side door, then in again to the other corridor in the front of the barn, and from there into her new stall. I placed two fingers on the number on the stall door.

"See—Number One. That's you."

She stuck her muzzle on the number. I couldn't tell whether it was because she understood what I was saying or because she wanted to taste the salt my fingers had left there.

We went in.

When I unsnapped the lead and came back out into the corridor alone, Mom was already hauling Bor along. "You know how *what* happened?"

"How Agora got pregnant. I bet it was at the Perseids shower last summer. When we were lying on the blanket, I saw something strange."

"Stranger than falling stars?" Mom stopped in front of me, Bor's huge head nuzzling her ear.

"I saw a light leaping the fence and then Agora ran to greet it and . . ."

"You," Mom said, pushing her finger in my chest, "*you* were fast asleep during the whole light show."

"Was not."

"Was," she said, and Bor nodded his head in punctuation. "I finally had to wake you up so we could go back inside." She pushed past me and led Bor into his stall.

I knew I hadn't been asleep. That couldn't be true. I vividly remembered what I'd seen. Even wrote about it in my journal the next day. I don't often write in my journal. Only if something interesting's happened. Like a spelling bee. Or a light show in the sky.

Or . . . a centaur.

Tonight's journal, I thought, *is going to be a doozy.*

"Then what's *your* explanation?" I called after her, sassier than I meant to, but not by much.

She stuck her head out of Bor's new stall. "I don't have one. Yet. When I do, it won't be about magic. It will be science-based."

"But it has to be magic," I said. "What else could it be?"

She didn't hear me because she was already back in the stall, and I could hear her murmuring to Bor. I suppose he was nuzzling her ear again, or making needy noises. Geldings are supposed to be these great big mountains of calm. But not Bor. Sometimes he acts like a big tough stallion, and other times just like a scared little kid.

This was one of the other times.

5

Eavesdropping

"We settled them in record time, despite their jitters," Mom said to Martha.

In answer, Martha just huffed through her nose like one of the horses. She does that sometimes instead of making a cutting comment.

Mom chose to ignore her and went toward the tack room to phone all the riders and boarders. "Got to tell them we have a situation here," she said.

"You're *not* telling," I called after her.

"*What* situation?" Martha growled at the same moment.

Mom stopped, turned, hands on hips. "I'm not spelling anything out, just saying we're under vet's orders to move all the horses to the front of the barn away from the new foal. That there's nothing to worry about for any of *their* horses. They can come on Wednesday when things will be up and running smoothly again. That gives us four full days."

I thought about those four days and a bubble of panic rose up into my throat as sharp as stomach acid.

"We'll have to expect some of them to be hysterical," Mom continued. "Some will probably try to come over today."

"The Angottis," Martha and I said together.

Mom nodded. "We'll tape off the back area and come up with a better explanation later, if needed. Gerry is driving over for lunch." And then she was gone.

"Gerry," I said softly, the way Mom had. Trying it out. Thinking of possible weddings and a dad.

"*Dr. Herks* to the likes of you and me," Martha said.

The wedding bubble burst. We had more important things to deal with.

☆ ☆ ☆

Martha told me to give the horses their water and new straw bedding, and to hand out apples and carrots as if it was a holiday. That took me the rest of the morning, since I had to do it by myself. Because instead of helping me,

Martha stayed in the stall with Agora and the foal and Robbie, who refused to leave.

Once I was done giving out horse treats, I went back to Agora's stall, knocked on the door, and waited till Martha grunted an invitation.

Robbie never takes naps, and yet he was fast asleep in his wheelchair, a blue horse blanket over him, pulled up around his neck. With his legs and arms covered, he looks just like any other six-year-old.

The pony boy was lying down with his head in Martha's lap. He had long, dark lashes, rosy cheeks, and a sprinkling of freckles over his nose. His hair was curly and thick, a roan's red.

"Martha," I whispered, "he's magic, isn't he?"

"Magic? I dunno. A bunch of trouble, more likely. All babies are. And heartache to come. But isn't he a little beaut."

And I suppose he was. Thumb in mouth, he was just as fast asleep as Robbie. If you didn't notice the horse part of him, the long, spindly legs, the hooves, the tail, the long barrel torso, he looked normal. Not a baby exactly, more like a toddler, as if he'd grown a year between when he was born earlier this morning and now.

Did I marvel at how fast that had happened? In a day of miracles, what was one miracle more?

☆ ☆ ☆

Later in the house, because he had to eat and then read his next assignment, Robbie complained about not being allowed back in the barn to see his "new brother."

"No," Mom said firmly.

Since he couldn't go out to the barn without someone helping him cross the gravel driveway, Robbie was stuck doing the last of his homework in the kitchen.

"It isn't fair," he began. "Ari doesn't have any homework today—"

Mom cut him off. "Ari has chores." She didn't point out that I didn't have any school in the summer. Since she schooled Robbie year-round, and not just during school term, it was better to let that issue alone. Teaching him throughout the year gave her more time for the farm each day and kept him busy. Usually that suited them both fine.

But not this time. And an hour later, when Dr. Herks arrived carrying two shopping bags full of our quarantine outfits, Robbie tried to complain to him.

"I agree with your mom, kiddo."

"Rats!" Robbie said, which was not like him at all. "Nobody cares about *me*."

"Pitiful you," I whispered, making my thumb and forefinger cross as if playing a miniature violin.

★ ★ ★

Martha came back in for lunch. That meant I was supposed to go take her place in Agora's stall, suited up and feeling like an idiot. Robbie had insisted on being pushed into his room, where he was probably sulking. Since sulking was not his way at all, it made us all extra edgy.

Dr. Herks said he'd have lunch back at his office because he had to perform emergency surgery on a border collie. "The rest of my afternoon's patients I'm leaving in the hands of my two assistants and Dr. Small," he told us.

Dr. Small was his veterinary partner, and the one thing she wasn't was tiny. But she was terrific with little animals, so in a way, her name fit her, while Dr. Herks handled most of the large animal stuff like horses and cows. Once—so he said—he delivered a baby elephant in Vietnam. I didn't know whether to believe him.

Then the grown-ups all started talking business stuff, like grain prices and how much we actually owed Dr.

Herks for the delivery since the foal had already been born when he arrived, and would he take payment in *increments*—a word I knew from a spelling bee, meaning little bits at a time.

All of a sudden, Mom said, "Go check on the barn, Ari," in a voice that offered no room for discussion, so I left.

But about halfway across the gravel drive, I suddenly had a strange feeling in the pit of my stomach and I tip-toed back to the kitchen door to eavesdrop, just in case they were making plans without me.

Sure enough, the three of them were discussing the next steps for keeping the pony boy safe. Mom and Martha often talk about important business matters without me, believing a thirteen-year-old doesn't need to know that stuff. And usually they're right. But I was seriously ticked off at Dr. Herks for joining them this time, especially because this was about the most important thing that had ever happened to us.

I could understand keeping the difficult business from Robbie, who was only six after all, and not able to help even when he wants to. But I was a big part of what makes the farm a success and now that something truly magical had happened, I was being treated like an out-sider.

☆ ☆ ☆

The trouble with listening in on a conversation you aren't supposed to hear is that you often find out stuff you never wanted to know. And once heard, no amount of wishing can make you unhear it.

Mom said, "I've been thinking about moving Agora and the foal—"

But Martha interrupted. "First he needs a name. A boy's name."

"Focus, Martha, focus," Mom scolded.

"I'm *always* focused. *On the horses.* And that boy needs a name."

That's when Dr. Herks said, "I think Hannah means we have to make him safe first, Martha. So how do we accomplish that?"

Martha said in that particular way she had, "Miz Martins told me she wondered about putting Aggie and the pony boy in the old washroom at the back of the house. But it's not nearly big enough, so somebody'd have to build it bigger. Hire somebody, and the secret would be all over town by lunchtime."

"Well, maybe I could board them both at the clinic's barn. I've got extra space where large animals stay after surgery."

"Gerry, would you?" I could hear soft hope in Mom's voice for the first time.

"And *then* how many people would be in on the secret?" Martha said.

Dr. Herks' grumbling answer came instantaneously. "My assistants to begin with and . . . Dr. Small, but I can vouch for them. We're used to keeping secrets about our patients."

"Ha!" Martha said. "Secrets like what cat has cancer and what dog can't keep control of its bowels—"

"Well, Aunty Dark Cloud," Mom said to Martha, "what would *you* have us do?"

I could hear the scrape of a chair. Martha must have stood up. "Since you've asked, I say close down the farm and send the horses that aren't ours back home with their owners while we figure this all out. That'd be the only sensible and sure way to keep him secret. And safe."

"You *know*, Martha, what keeps this farm running is the money we get from boarding other people's horses and giving their kids riding lessons. Every penny I have is invested in the farm, and the small check Wolf sends goes to pay off the mortgage. How would we eat or pay your salary or—"

"Hah! Wolf. That what he calls himself now? Lesley wasn't good enough?"

"Ladies," Dr. Herks said calmly, "we need to have a Plan A for dealing with things right now and a Plan B for when this gets out. Because like it or not, it's only a matter of time before the secret is blown."

I thought about going back inside, though it would mean they'd all know I'd been listening in. I even put my hand on the doorknob.

Dr. Herks ended lamely, "We can't keep him hidden forever."

"We can try!"

"Martha, we have to be realistic," Mom said.

I was listening so hard at this point, I was breaking out in a sweat.

"What's *real* here, Miz Martins, is that little newborn out in the barn. And the fact that you and me and Ari work so hard to keep the place running while that Lesley slithered out from under as soon as he could, not wanting to have anything to do with his poor little son that he called a monster, leaving you with nothing but the farm. You know all that, Dr. Herks? Well, there's a tale I could tell."

"Wolf? Lesley?"

Mom said softly, "My ex."

"And good riddance to the bad rubbish. He was mean as a snake and about as trustworthy."

"Martha!" Mom's voice got a bit muzzy. "He was sweet a lot of the time. And in the beginning, well, he loved me."

"When he wanted something," Martha said, "he was sweet then like cotton candy at the state fair, make you choke on the sweetness. Full of love then, till he got what he wanted. And I ask no forgiveness for saying this, and I make no apologies."

That's when Mom's voice got hard, her no-nonsense voice. "Apologies or not, don't you ever talk about Arianne and Robbie's father like that if they're in the room."

"Well, they aren't in the room now, Miz Martins. But that doesn't change that snake's skin. *Snake*, whether he's sweet-talking or not."

I could just imagine their faces.

Hmmm . . . . that was the sound of Dr. Herks clearing his throat. "So, Martha," he said, "what would you have *me* do about him, about the pony boy?"

"Keep him secret. Keep him safe. Give him a chance to grow up, poor little mite."

Dr. Herks' voice got soft, as if he'd turned to look at Mom. "And what about you, Hannah?"

"Do?" she started and then her voice began to run downhill. "What do I want you to *do*? I don't . . . I don't know." She started to cry quietly. And I hadn't heard her cry since . . . well, since forever.

I tiptoed away, but as I walked to the barn, I thought, *We're all taking baby steps here. Shakily, slowly. And someone— maybe everyone—is going to fall down.*

6

Four Days

THE REST OF THE DAY WAS CHAOS. Mom had already called everyone who was boarding a horse or riding, and she only had to leave messages with two maids. The two boarders who called back wanted to make sure:

1. It wasn't a prank call.
2. Their horses weren't in danger.
3. They didn't have to move their horses to a more expensive farm.
4. Riding lessons would continue after the short break.

Everyone agreed to give us the four days' grace, so Mom relented and let Robbie have an hour in Agora's stall watching the pony boy sleep.

"Why does he sleep so much?" Robbie asked me when I'd pushed him in. "I want to play with him."

"Babies sleep a lot," I said, reminding him how he'd been when Mom brought him back from the hospital. "All day and hardly at all at night."

"Then I want to be here at night, too."

"Mom will never allow it."

He knew that was true and didn't say a word more about it.

☆ ☆ ☆

I left him in the stall and then put four sawhorses across the driveway. Mom said it was to prevent anyone else possibly trying to come in.

For the first three days the sawhorses worked.

For those three days, I balked at wearing the quarantine outfit. It was too big, and I kept tripping on the long pants. I hated the mask.

But I kept the outfit close. We just didn't know when someone might show up.

Surprisingly, no one did.

Oh, we still got mail, and one package, and a grain delivery. But Mom managed to keep them from coming anywhere near the barn, even though we had to haul the grain in from the front porch ourselves.

"Breathing space," Martha called it. None of us expected it to last any longer than that.

And honestly, with the extra amount of barn work I now had, mucking out the additional stalls, I wasn't sure I wanted it to last any longer. But we had no other option but to try for more time.

We did get occasional help from Dr. Herks, who checked in every day and never balked at picking up a hammer or taking a turn with the oats buckets or straw bedding. He had hauled most of the sacks of grain in the wheelbarrow. It helped that there was a ramp off the porch for Robbie's wheelchair. But the rest of the work was done by Mom and Martha and me.

☆ ☆ ☆

On that first day, Mom and Martha strengthened the barriers to Agora's new stall. Instead of blankets for the windows, Dr. Herks bought blinds at a shop in Springfield, which Martha hung on the inside of the windows. At the same time, Dr. Herks put up spotlights, a new lock, and an inside bolt. The lock had five sets of keys.

The next day, Martha gave us lanyards she'd made for the keys, all in different colors. Hers was deep blue, Mom's yellow, mine pink, Robbie's light blue, and Dr. Herks' green.

"If a key goes missing," she told us, "we'll know by its color."

"We'll know because the person who lost it will be looking for it," Dr. Herks said, flapping his arms and pretending to be panicked.

Martha glared at him with a face that could turn a man to stone.

I was reading a book of Greek myths whenever it was my turn on foal watch. I needed to find out what I could about centaurs. It had these great paintings in full color, so real-looking it was as if the artist had taken a photograph of the characters, not just made them up from his imagination. I knew—from a unit in fourth grade—that centaurs were mythical horse-human creatures from Greece. However, this wasn't ancient Greece, and our pony boy was very real. It also seemed odd that magic should need us to be so practical: locks and keys, floodlights and blinds—and books. But we had to make our pony boy safe in this unmagical world.

I also figured that if he needed a name, I knew where I'd find one.

There were four pages on centaurs in the book, which I'd all but memorized. I read part of it aloud to Robbie.

I also learned a new word—*liminal*, which means something caught between two different natures: like someone between life and death, or someone who is both horse and man. Or a werewolf. Or a faun. Or—I thought—someone like me, not quite a grown-up, not quite a kid. That's liminal.

Also, it was a great spelling word.

Turns out, the Greek centaurs weren't very nice at all. I'd forgotten that. In fact, they sounded sort of like a gang—dragging girls away from weddings, beating up people, rioting in town centers. There was only one really good centaur, named Chiron. He was a teacher whose students included the heroes Jason and Achilles. Also there was Pholus, who was described as "civilized," which made him sound like a snob. And Nessus. I liked his name best, but he was *really* evil and helped kill Hercules with a poisoned shirt. I sure didn't want to name our foal Nessus. He already had enough bad luck just being born into our world.

"So, what do you think?" I asked Robbie the third day of our four-day grace period. We were taking a three-hour shift, and I'd just been reading the centaur stories out loud to him. *Again*. Robbie could read on his own, but he loved the way I acted out the tales, hopping about like a crazed centaur or shaking my finger as Chiron might have done to his centaur students. Like Dad used to do to me.

Agora ignored me, but the pony boy listened intently, fascinated as the stories unfolded, almost as if he could understand them. His eyes were bright, a clear swimming-pool blue, and his head swiveled back and forth as he listened to each one of us in turn.

"How about Pholus?" I asked Robbie.

He shook his head. "Sounds too much like *Fool*."

"What about Chiron?" That was my new favorite name.

"We could call him Kai!" Robbie said excitedly.

At that, the pony boy's mouth dropped open as if he knew we were talking about him. He held out his left hand, palm up, the right one being plugged into his mouth by its thumb. Then he put his head to one side considering us, or the name, or the world of his stall, before trotting over to

Robbie. He no longer had the unfinished look of a new-born human, for he already had begun this phenomenal growth spurt. Like most three-day-old colts, he was still a bit unsteady on those legs, and he nearly pushed Robbie out of his wheelchair.

I stepped in between them and raised my hands. "Whoa there, Buster. Too bad brakes don't come with that body."

"Not Buster—*Kai*!" Robbie reminded me.

Kai took the thumb out of his mouth and laughed out loud. "Kai!" he said, as perfect as that.

Robbie whooped. "He said it! He said his name!"

Talking at three days? Now *that's* magic!

"Kai it is, then." I put my hand to my chest. "Ari," I said.

It took three times before he got it. He poked me in the chest. "Awee."

Close enough, I thought.

Robbie gestured toward his own chest. Poking was too hard for his little arms. "Robbie!"

Kai laughed. "Wobbie." And then he looked at me. "Awee." Then he jabbed at his own chest. "Kai." He said all three again quickly, as if it was a chant. "Awee, Wobbie, Kai." Then his head went back and he laughed delightedly.

I put my right arm around his shoulders and gave him a gentle hug, as tentative as I'd been with Robbie when he was little, so afraid that with all his medical problems, I might break something important.

Kai threw both arms around me, his hug awkward and much too strong for a three-day-old. I could feel his heart beating.

His little boy heart. And the horse heart, too.

Enough love there, I thought, *for all of us.*

The Angotti Factor

THOSE FIRST THREE DAYS WENT BY much too quickly, like the lead horse racing at the Three County Fairground. All we managed to get done in that time was to name Kai and make his stall as safe as possible. The rest of the time, we had all the other horses to take care of, Robbie's school-work, and Dr. Herks' careful monitoring of Kai's extra-ordinary growth.

Extraordinary was Mom's word. I just thought, *Wow! Is he getting big fast!*

It was as if the boy part of his body had to grow extra quick to keep up with the horse part. In those first few days, he got more and more control of his legs, grew baby teeth, and learned to put a few words together to make sentences, something it would take a regular human kid a year or more to do.

He developed muscles in his upper arms by pushing at the stall door whenever we left and never got that pouchy baby tummy that some of my little cousins had.

Along with the growth, his hair grew in red-brown tendrils till it was halfway down his neck. He looked so adorable, I took three pictures of him with Mom's Polaroid camera. I showed them to him, and he said, "Who that, Awee?"

"Silly," Robbie said. "It's you."

Kai looked puzzled. He didn't understand how different he was. I mean, how could he? He was still a baby in many ways.

So I asked Mom if we could get a mirror for him.

The next time Dr. Herks came to check on Kai, he brought along a narrow full-length mirror and mounted it on the barn door.

Kai spent hours looking at himself in the mirror, playing peekaboo games, until he finally realized that the interesting pony boy there was himself.

As for the photographs, I pinned them to my bedroom bulletin board.

Mom called Kai's growth spurt a miracle. Martha called it a marvel. Dr. Herks called it nature, nurture, and myth combining.

I—the one person who had wanted magic in our lives—seemed to be the one person worried that it was going to mean more trouble for us. Meaning me.

Only Robbie fully accepted the magic that was Kai.

Oh—and Agora, of course. Since she'd never had a foal before, perhaps she just thought this was an ordinary birth, an ordinary foal, an ordinary boy.

☆ ☆ ☆

The four days we asked our horse boarders to give us should have been enough. But we hadn't counted on Mrs. Angotti's sneaky determination. She kept calling Mom and getting put off again and again. So she took things into her own hands.

The morning of the next day, she didn't call ahead, just arrived without announcing her intentions at a time when Martha and I were mucking out stalls, Robbie was in with Agora and Kai, and Mom was in the house making phone calls.

The Angottis—Mrs. A and the two kids, Joey and Angela—all got out to shift the sawhorses so they could drive right up to the barn.

I saw them by accident as I started out of the stables

and would have said something, but Mom had already seen them, too. She came galloping out of the house, waving her hands to stop them. So I shrank back against the wall.

She and Mrs. A argued for about five minutes, most of the time loud enough for me to hear.

Halfway through, Mom said, "I'll go and get your horses right now and tie them to the back of your car if you drive up to the barn."

Mrs. A replied, "You wouldn't!"

"Just try me! They can trot home after you, or you can leave them here, but you're *not* coming in. Not till the four days are up and the vet gives us the all clear. Maybe even longer."

They were still arguing when I sneaked back to Agora's stall. Robbie was reading a book to himself while Kai slept. Agora was quietly munching on grain.

I got into one of the green quarantine suits and put the mask on.

Just in case.

"Stay here," I whispered so I didn't wake Kai.

Robbie dropped the book about Thomas Jefferson into his lap and stared at me.

"And put on Martha's suit just in case. Mask, too."

They were hanging on the back of the door. I handed them to him. He could just about manage without me.

"Why . . . ?"

"The Angottis are here."

"But it's not four days yet," he whined.

"I know that. But they're here anyway."

At that moment Agora made an odd sound, and I turned to see her straddling her sleeping foal and baring her teeth at the door.

It didn't take a horse whisperer to guess something was up.

Agora never acted this way except when one of the Angottis was around. I don't know that they're actually *bad* kids. But they're loud, and they always seem to find trouble.

As a four-year-old, Joey had spilled out a week's worth of oats onto the muddy area by the barn door to make something he called "horse poo!" He also poured his Coke into Bor's water trough because he felt sorry that Bor only had water to drink.

One time before a horse show at the Three County Fair, Angela plaited Marzipan's forelock so tightly, the poor thing was cross-eyed with a headache for a week.

Martha finally had to cut the forelock short because trying to unwind it would take too much time and hurt Marzipan even more.

Of course, Mrs. Angotti blamed us for everything. She said we should have had a proper lock on the oats. Bor's stall should have been out of the reach of children. And she was *apoplectic*—Mom's word, but I love it and even learned to spell it—when Martha "damaged Marzipan forever by cutting off her hair."

"Somebody explain to her that that hair grows back," Martha muttered as she walked away. "I can't be bothered."

But now Agora was practically growling. If Agora was upset about one of the Angottis, the problem had to be dealt with—and fast.

So, in the quarantine suit and mask, I went to the doorway of the stall, lifted the shade over the window, and peeked out.

Sure enough, there was Joey sneaking down the corridor. I opened the stall door, then closed and locked it behind me. In my surgical gear—now a bit dirty from sitting on the floor—I gave him quite a fright.

"Jeez Louise," he said, "who are you?"

I took the mask off. "It's me, Arianna. And why are you *here*? Haven't you been told this part of the barn's off-limits?"

"What does that mean?" He actually looked innocent saying that, which made me wonder.

"It means you're not allowed here. Not for *any* reason at all. We've got sick horses that you just can't be around."

"Whatcha dressed like that for?" His nose wrinkled as if he'd smelled something awful.

I pointed to the two signs, the one that said QUARITINE in Martha's block writing and the poster board where it was spelled right.

"What does *that* mean?" He went up close to the signs and sounded out the words, pronouncing them wrong. "Quart-een."

"It means no one goes in or out without the proper clothes and proper mask."

"I could do that."

I had to think of something to really discourage him. "And you have to take a special bath with carbolic soap that stings something fierce and raises prickles all over your body."

"Eeeeeew," he said.

"Because," and now I was really getting into it, "while we think what the horses have isn't catching, the vet says we've got to be *super* careful. You know, people catching a horse sickness wouldn't be pretty. In fact, it could actually be . . ." I stopped, looked around as if making sure no one was listening, leaned toward him, and whispered, "Life threatening."

For the first time he seemed uncertain. "Which horses? I hope it's not Bor."

Bor was his favorite.

Bor didn't think much of Joey.

"Agora and her new foal."

"She's not a horse. She's a *pony*," he said, as if that made her worthless.

This wasn't the time to argue with him. Besides, arguing with an Angotti is like arguing with a pack of mules, or so Martha says. "Only without having a two-by-four handy."

"Can I see from out here?" Joey said. "I won't touch anything."

"No, you can't."

He made a face.

"I *mean* it, Joey." I may be one of the shortest kids in my class, but I'm a good foot taller than Joey, who's only in third grade.

He shrugged and walked back the way he came.

I should have been suspicious when he gave up that easily, but I was just relieved he'd gone. As soon as he turned the corner, I went back into Agora's stall.

Just as I sat down, I heard a noise at the door, and the blinds twitched.

"Jeeze Louise!"

I looked at Joey's face peering through the blinds and jumped between Agora and his sightline, hoping I'd been fast enough. Then I stomped up to the door, opened it a crack, and sidled outside.

Grabbing Joey by the arm, I yanked him away from the door.

"What did you see," I demanded. "What did you *see?*"

He looked up at me, eyes wide with fright. "You weren't wearing your mask in there," he whimpered. "And then you came out here and touched me. Am I going to get what they have? Am I gonna have prickles all over my body? Am I gonna *die?*" He started to wail, though tears never actually came into his eyes.

I gave him a push toward the end of the corridor. "Get

out! Go away!" I shouted. "Or I'll tell your mother on you. In fact, I might just tell her anyway!" I screamed the last word. And I shook my fist at him.

He ran around the corner and this time was gone for good.

I was shaking so hard, I thought I might throw up. I ran back to the stall window and twitched the blind to see what Joey might have seen.

Agora was now on her side, her big bottom mounded up. Behind her Kai was still fast asleep. The only parts of him showing were his little hind legs, which stuck out beyond hers.

Going back into the stall, my legs wobbled even more than Kai's had ever done, only mine were wobbling from fright. If Joey or any of the Angottis hurt Kai, I knew I'd . . . I'd . . . but I couldn't think what I could do. I simply locked the door from the inside, then sat down to look at Agora and Kai as they slept. My mind was a blank until I remembered how strong Kai's hug had been.

"Just give us a few more days," I said, a kind of prayer. I knew as a good Quaker, one shouldn't pray for special gifts but rather pledge to do something special for someone else, something hard. But this *was* for someone else, I reasoned. It was for Kai.

I didn't want to wait till Mom came for me. Standing, I said to Robbie, "I'm going to lock you in with Agora and Kai and go tell Mom what just happened."

"What happened?" he said. "What?"

"Joey Angotti happened," I said. "Kai was almost seen."

"That's not good," he said. "Lock me in, skipper."

I ran out of the stall and locked it, pocketing the key.

As I rounded the side of the barn, I placed the mask over my mouth again and started shouting. "Mom, Mom, Joey was just—"

Mrs. Angotti took one look at me, then shouted at her kids, "Get back in the car and don't let me hear a word from either one of you until we're down the road."

Joey jumped in the back seat, but Angela was a bit slower on the uptake, though she wasn't far behind. Then Mrs. Angotti got in on the driver's side, started the car, reversed it, and they drove away in a spray of gravel.

As they went around the first curve and disappeared from sight, Mom turned. She was wiping her eyes.

I ran to her and put my arms around her. "What's wrong—what did she say? Was it awful?"

"Lord, you're an amazing daughter," Mom said. "Sometimes I think you're older than I am. You're certainly smarter. But not this time."

Then I realized she was laughing.

"The expression on Mrs. Angotti's face when you came out in your . . ." Mom began laughing again and wiping her eyes. Then she turned serious. "We have a lot to do. But, Lord! I needed that laugh."

"About time," Martha said, as she came out of the other side of the barn. Evidently, she'd heard the whole thing and she spit the two words out like bullets after their departing car. Then she added, "Ya think she'll come back for her two horses?"

We all walked back to Agora's stall together.

"Well, we never liked them anyway," I said.

"That's not the issue, Ari." Mom shook her head. "Nor a very Quakerly thing to say. The Angottis have been loyal to us when they could have gone elsewhere. And they have lots of cousins, some of whom have been promising to come riding. We need every boarder and rider we have, and we really need to keep them whether we like them or not. They pay the bills."

I knocked on the door. "Robbie," I said, "it's me and Mom and Martha." Then I opened the door and peered in.

Just then Kai awoke, made a funny little sound, and started to stand. Agora headed right over to nuzzle him.

He must have grown in his sleep because he was

already close to Agora's size. She didn't seem to notice, or if she noticed, she didn't seem to mind.

I heard Mom draw in a quick breath. And Martha said, "That's no growth spurt, that's a growth geyser!"

"What's a geyser?" Robbie asked.

"An upside-down waterfall, pipsqueak," Martha said.

"But waterfalls can't fall up."

"We've named him," I said, partly to change the subject, partly to get back into the conversation. "Chiron. He was the good centaur, a teacher, in the Greek myths. But that's too long and hard a name for our little guy, so Robbie suggested calling him Kai. Pony boy seems to like it."

"Robbie told me."

"Oh." So much for my surprise. "Do *you* like it?"

"Well," Mom joked, "if it's a myth-stake, it's a good one!"

"Myth-stake?" I repeated and then, all of a sudden, I snorted through my nose.

Mom put her hand to her mouth and began to giggle uncontrollably, and I got the giggles as well. We went on like that for almost a minute, before she took a deep breath and picked a piece of straw from Kai's long tendrils of hair.

He smiled at her, which made him look like one of the old paintings from the Greek myth book. "Tank, Mom."

"Thank you, Mom," she said.

"Thank you, Mom," he repeated. I knew he wouldn't forget how to say it now.

"We need to get a brush through this mop, Ari."

That's when I felt things would be all right, with or without the Angottis, because Mom and I were laughing together and talking about regular stuff and accepting the magic, too.

But I was wrong.

Uncovered Story

FOR ABOUT A WEEK MORE, THE COVER STORY HELD. No one but us dared go near the quarantine stall, even after all the riders returned.

Well, not all—the Angottis stayed home, leaving a friend—who also boarded her gelding at our stable—to comb and curry and feed their horse, plus change out the bedding and muck out her stall.

No one wanted me or Mom or Martha or even Dr. Herks near their horses. Just in case.

We had a swarm of vets come from as far away as Connecticut to check out the boarders' horses. Sneakily, Dr. Herks managed to keep them away from Agora and Kai. I'm not sure what he told them. It had to be quite a spin on things because he couldn't fool them with his diagnosis of *Puericentaurcephal-whatsis*. Still, whatever he said seemed to work, and for the time being, we all breathed a sigh of relief.

However, it quickly became clear that, sooner or later—and probably sooner—our boarders were going to take their horses elsewhere. And their kids were going to go elsewhere for lessons as well. Which would mean the farm would go broke, and we'd have to move. And . . . well, I couldn't bear thinking about the rest.

By Thursday, the first of the riders who didn't own their own horses began leaving. And Friday some of the owners came to collect their horses, including Patti and her dad, and she didn't even come over to say good-bye. My standing at the end of Agora's corridor in my quarantine suit, arms folded, mask on, might have had something to do with that, but she could have waved.

As far as the rest of them, well, as Mom said, "Some have been kind enough to let us know," meaning they'd phoned before showing up to get their horses or their tack. Others simply never showed up again. Like Maddi and her mom, who just sent someone else for their horse and stuff.

We were down ten riders and five horses by Friday evening, not counting our own.

Through the weekend, we waved good-bye to about

half of the other riders. Worried about the remaining horses not getting ridden enough, Martha made a schedule, and Mom and I took turns on solo trail rides. We couldn't go together. Someone had to guard Kai. Someone besides Robbie, that is. He spent hours in Agora's stall, playing simple games with Kai, reading to him, sometimes just sitting there with his arm around Kai's neck, teaching him new words like *brother, funny bone, carrots,* and *rain.*

☆ ☆ ☆

When we took the horses on the trail, they seemed more angry than upset, and startled at the smallest things. Bor almost unseated me, and in return, I was rough on his mouth, sawing with the reins, something I never did with him. Hera was so skittish, I had to turn her around and walk her home, letting her run free for about an hour in the paddock before conning her to go back into the barn, not with just one but two apples and a carrot, plus sugar as a sweetener.

Even I understood we couldn't go on like this.

I caught Mom staring at herself in the hallway mirror, her right pointer finger touching the dark circles under her eyes. When I tried to put my arms around her, she shrugged me off. She held whispered conversations over the phone with Dr. Herks.

After three days of this, we all got snarky with one another, saying things we didn't mean. I called Mom selfish, which she certainly wasn't. Martha snapped out one-liners as if she was shooting at moving targets. Mom told her to shut up and shape up, which worked for about an hour, and then Martha was at it again.

Robbie, normally the sunniest of us all, would cry and slam doors whenever he had to leave Kai. One door caught his wheelchair at a bad angle and tipped him over, which brought on even more tears and a trip to the doctor's.

With Mom and Robbie at the doctor's, I said something about being overprotective of him to Martha, who called me "a pony princess with neither the grace to be a princess nor the brains to be a pony." I ran out of the barn rather than cry in front of her.

Martha found me an hour later in Agora's stall, dressed in the quarantine suit but without the mask, and apologized in her strange way.

"You know," she said, squinting at me, "you do have some grace, Ari. And I bet you're just about as smart as a pony, especially in school. Just don't be a smart aleck, that's all."

We nodded at each other, but there was little warmth in it.

Or forgiveness.

☆ ☆ ☆

Martha and I still had to work together, since we shared most of the barn chores. Now that we had fewer horses and riders, those chores were lightened considerably.

Robbie did what he could, though honestly, he was in the way most of the time and cranky when any of us began to push him back to the house.

"My brother, my turn," he'd protest, his face pinched and unhappy. I think it was more than that. He'd never had a friend before—except me—and he was possessive of that friendship in a fierce way.

One time he even turned in his chair as I was wheeling him out of the stall, reaching one of his shortened arms toward Kai. And Kai wailed back, trotting to the door to call out, "Robbie, come back. Now!"

I tried to argue Robbie out of his temper and his sadness, but Martha was tougher, giving him a stern warning. "If someone hears you whining, Squinch, the game's up."

"What game?"

"The quarantine game, kiddo. There are two little boys in the stall. Something won't add up."

After that, all she had to say if he got even slightly cranky was "game's up, kiddo," and he'd stop fussing.

Unfortunately, that never worked for me.

Meanwhile, Mom had become curiously quiet, almost sleepwalking through the day. She hardly talked to anyone, unless she was asked a direct question. Her eyes had raccoon circles under them, and she looked like she was losing weight. I worried about her. But I didn't know what to do, and I sure didn't want to get shrugged off again.

On the Friday morning of the third week, I found Mom fast asleep in Kai's stall, his head cradled in the crook of her arm. If I squinted my eyes and didn't focus on the rest of him, he looked completely human. Mom had covered up the boy half of him with one of Robbie's old baby blankets.

"Mom," I said, into her ear so as not to disturb Kai. It reminded me of happier times, when I would wander into the room where she and Dad slept, and I'd crawl in on her side. Waking Dad was out of the question. He stayed out very late at night playing in rock clubs. Mom used to say that not even the atom bomb would get him up.

Mom looked up, her eyes muzzy with sleep. Then she smiled. I remembered that smile from when she first came home from the hospital with Robbie.

Before Dad left.

"Were you here all night?" I asked.

"Protection," she said, "just in case." Then she glanced at her watch. "Oh my goodness. Look at the time. Go get Martha up."

But Martha was already at the door, saying, "I told you she needed to know."

"Needed to know what?"

"Needed to know that you've got an early dentist appointment," Mom said, standing carefully and brushing the straw off her clothes. "Wanted to get it in before anyone comes for a horse. So, go grab something from the pantry for breakfast and make sure Robbie is up—"

"Why didn't you *tell* me?" I demanded. We both knew I wasn't talking about the dentist but about her sleeping all night in the stall. "What if Robbie had an emergency and I couldn't find you? What if . . ." I stopped for a second, then plowed on. "What if *I* had an emergency?"

"You never do," she said gently. "And if you did, you'd solve it yourself. You never let me in."

"Still . . ."

"I just forgot," she said, blushing. She wasn't someone who lied easily. It made hiding Kai extra hard on her.

"I'll drive her," Martha said. "And do some grocery shopping while she's getting checked out. We're low on everything. I checked your pantry and fridge."

"Thanks," Mom said, knowing full well I would pump Martha for answers, and Martha would give them to me.

☆ ☆ ☆

In the car, Martha told me everything I wanted to know and some things I didn't. How there were only five riders left, with horse vans coming to transport the last of the boarding horses to nearby stables that very afternoon. How our various suppliers of oats and straw were demanding immediate full payment. How Mr. Suss from next door had made a low offer for our farm, so low it was laughable. How the Angottis were threatening to sue us.

"I think we should sue them for . . ." Martha thought a minute. "Well, just for being the Angottis!"

"How come I wasn't told any of this before?"

"Because your mom is treating you like a kid," she said, her eyes on the road, which was just as well. Martha is a terrible driver.

"I *am* a kid."

"Don't be a sassy-pants. You've never been a kid. You were born a grown-up." She turned to glare at me, and the car took a slight bobble to the right.

I shrank back in my seat.

"Since Kai's been born, she's afraid all the time for you. And for Robbie. She's protecting you."

"I don't need protecting," I said. "But Robbie does."

At least she was looking at the road again.

"She's your mom. She's supposed to protect *both* of you."

After that there was silence.

When we arrived at the dentist's building, I got out and refused to turn to say good-bye. I was angry. Angry with the boarders and riders for being unkind; angry with Mr. Suss, who was a thief; angry with Martha and Mom for keeping things secret; angry with Dr. Herks, who seemed to have stopped being there for us; angry with

Robbie for needing help when we were already stretched too thin; angry with myself for being too young to be a real help—even angry with Agora, who got herself pregnant and . . .

Well, at least I wasn't angry with Kai.

9

Freak of Nature

ON THE DRIVE HOME, my lips still tingling from the Novocain, my tongue exploring the two new fillings, I refused to speak to Martha. But if I didn't talk to her, who *could* I talk to? Patti and Maddi were already gone, and besides, I never really said very much to either of them. Even if I wanted to, how could I have explained what was happening at the farm? How could I have trusted them with our secret?

My tongue found the fillings again, and at that I began to wonder what Kai would be eating after he was weaned off his mother's milk—once he lost all his baby teeth, and all the adult teeth came in. Given how fast he was growing, that might be any day now.

Horses eat grass and oats mixed with peas and beans and lentils. For treats they get carrots, apples—our horses love McIntosh the most—and the occasional sugar lump. But that's not a growing *boy*'s diet.

Mom always drilled that into me—every day something protein, something green, a grain, a piece of fruit, and milk. My lunches at school had been boring. No one in elementary school ever wanted to share. I mean who would take celery sticks over a candy bar? Or trade a chocolate chip cookie for a box of raisins?

Dr. Herks hadn't said a word about Kai's diet, which was odd. Made me wonder about our pony boy's stomach. We knew he had two hearts. But what if he had two different stomachs as well?

I supposed Kai could be fed vegan. Both my aunts, Dad's sisters, were in the Vegan Society. No eggs or fish or butter or any kind of meat at all. Come to think of it, Aunt May ate a lot like a horse: oversalted vegetables and dandelions she picked in her yard. Dad used to tease her about it and offer her bites of his hamburger whenever she came to visit. Aunt May would sniff angrily, but his other sister, Aunt Ella, would burst into tears. We hadn't seen either of them in years. Not since Dad left.

☆ ☆ ☆

By the time Martha and I got home, I expected to see trailers in the driveway and owners collecting their horses. I was surprised that there were only two cars: the Angottis' blue van and Dr. Herks' truck.

Martha parked her car by the little cottage, but instead of putting away her groceries, she headed straight for the farmhouse, probably to report to Mom.

Not me. I ran into the barn, wondering if they'd all changed their minds about coming to collect the horses. Or else maybe they'd already been and gone while I was at the dentist.

But once in the barn, I discovered all the horses were still where they belonged.

Curiouser and curiouser.

I went to the other side of the barn to check on Kai.

No one was standing by Agora's stall, which was locked. But with the Angottis around, why wasn't somebody guarding the door?

I raced into the house, taking the back steps two at a time and getting to the kitchen just as Mrs. Angotti marched in through the front door. I could hear her voice three rooms away. Big and booming, like she had a megaphone.

"Yeah, I'm sorry I didn't knock," she was saying, "but the door was already open—well, at least not exactly locked—and besides, you need to explain something to me and to Joey here, because believe it or not, we got a really iffy situation, which may need some truly extra-careful unraveling, and I think you know what I mean! Because it's actually ruining your already sinking business and gave my little boy a huge scare! And I don't like anyone scaring my kids, nobody or nothing, so I think someone, maybe you or maybe the vet here, needs to give me a quick explanation—I'm not talking to Martha, because she's a sassy loudmouthed . . . ! Or your poor little boy."

Mrs. Angotti has a tendency to speak in run-on sentences, the kind my English teacher never lets us use in essays. It's rule number three on her first-day handout, right after *No exclamation marks* and *Watch that your adverbs don't propagate.*

Mrs. Angotti would flunk ninth-grade English. When she talks, it's an amazing thing to listen to, because she doesn't seem to breathe between sentences. ("Or even paragraphs," Mom says.) Also, she seems be in love with exclamation points, and she never met an adverb she didn't like.

Just as I ran into the room, Mom was saying, "Since

you're suing me, Maria, I shouldn't be talking to you without a lawyer present."

Mom and Dr. Herks were sitting close on the sofa, with a bunch of papers spread out on the coffee table. Martha was standing by the door as if she'd just closed it, but not soon enough. The look on her face sat somewhere between a worry and a thunderstorm. Holding an open book on his lap, Robbie was looking up angrily. He hated being pitied above anything else.

Mrs. Angotti had a grip on Joey's arm, like she was furious with him, but as she spoke, all her fury seemed to go outward in an unfocused way. Her hair was unfocused, too. Wiry, shot through with strands of white, it stood up around her head like she'd put her finger in an electric socket. She was wearing her usual jodhpurs.

Not that she ever got up on a horse. Martha thinks she's scared. Mom thinks she's allergic. I think the jodhpurs are a fashion statement.

Mrs. Angotti must have taken a deep breath, because she'd already started talking again, saying, "I didn't mean a real suit, with lawyers, I was just mortally piqued, you know, not the *p-e-a-k* kind of high-on-a-mountain sort of thing, but the I'm-mad-at-you pique and trying to get your attention since your attention seems to be totally wandering these days, because it's sure not on your riders and our horses, but I shouldn't have done it because, as Mr. Angotti always says, 'Don't threaten what you're not gonna do!'"

Martha rumbled, "Hold your horses, lady!"

That's when I noticed Joey's hair.

He has the same hair as his mother's, only without the white bits. This morning he had pieces of straw stuck on the left side, so he looked like he had the part of Scarecrow in a school play of *The Wizard of Oz.*

Straw, I thought, suddenly really worried.

Mrs. Angotti took another short breath. And then she was off again, speaking in that run-on way.

"So we up and came back here just to check on things, even though I'd already said we weren't coming back and Mr. Angotti said we should stay at home, but I knew Joey wanted to say good-bye to Bor, 'cause he dearly loves that horse so much, and Angela at first decided not to come, she has a boyfriend she needs to talk to twenty times a day, which ties up the phone line for hours! You should *see* the way she lies on the sofa and twists the cord up around her shoulder! But I told her that if we were gonna move her horse, that Marzipan, who sometimes acts like a snooty prom queen and needs our full attention, she had to be on board with it—Angela I mean, not Marzipan, who just needs a good pull and a slap on the behind, and she'll do as she's told, Marzipan I mean, not Angela, 'cause these days, even if I wanted to lift a hand to her, which I don't, I'd hardly get her to do anything if I got physical, which is what happened to my dad when he used his belt or the back of his hand on any of us, 'cause I can't actually move Marzipan alone, you know. And after Joey and I saw Bor—and by the way, that stall's not very clean, not your usual standard—I said we had to leave, and he said in a minute and took a carrot out of the bag and ran back, and I thought he was going to give it to Bor, on account of how much he loves that horse, but he's like his father and can't ever do what he's told or what he should, gets awfully distracted, you know—and suddenly he's back again with a face white as my mother-in-law's pasta—which is something *you* should try, put some real meat on those bones of yours, and on your girl, too—saying something about a freak!"

She took a big breath this time.

"He *didn't!*" I gasped. No one calls my brother names. And that was when everyone noticed me.

Mom was up on her feet, a hand to her mouth. Dr. Herks had gotten up, too, holding on to Mom's arm.

Martha had started forward toward Mrs. Angotti. And Robbie dropped his book on the floor, his face scrunched up as if he was trying hard not to cry.

But nothing was going to stop Mrs. A now. She was like a horse with the bit between its teeth.

"I should've," she said, "slapped him for fibbing, except the one thing Joey doesn't do is tell lies! He's not above really stretching the truth now and then for effect, only we call it storytelling, and as Mr. Angotti likes to say, 'Just because it isn't so doesn't mean it isn't true,' which makes sense the longer you think about it! So I let Joey lead me over to the other stall, the one that's quarantined—which is a strange word, but so are most *q* words, like *quince* and *quota*, which will get you a lot of points in Scrabble—and I looked where he was pointing in the stall when he twitched the blinds aside."

While I was puzzling over all these new revelations about Mrs. Angotti, as well as her sentence structure, Mom interjected, "You *didn't*!"

That was unfortunate, because it gave Mrs. Angotti the chance to take another really deep breath, and then she was off again, hands waving about as she talked.

"I did, and a good thing I did, too, since you've been saying all along it's some sort of disease, and lots of folks have already taken their horses away, though what they'll do now that it's a FREAK OF NATURE and not a disease, I don't really know, but that's certainly better than something that might be communicable—another great Scrabble word—but I don't know if everyone will feel the same way."

For a minute, I thought she meant she was wondering if anyone felt the same way about using the Scrabble word. And then *I got it*! She'd said "freak of nature" like it was all capital letters. She wasn't talking about *Robbie*. Joey had known Robbie for the past four years, and even Mrs. Angotti would never have let him call Robbie such a name.

She was talking about Kai.

Dr. Herks leaned toward her, two hundred pounds of angry vet, speaking in a cold, controlled voice that even I could tell was just on the ragged edge of losing it. "Have you *said* anything to anyone?"

Since Mrs. Angotti, according to Martha, has no off button and only an on button, that was the *only* question to ask.

Martha didn't lean in like Dr. Herks, but if anything, she was angrier. "Who . . . else . . . knows?" Each word was like a bullet to the heart. A strange image for a Quaker girl to use, I know, but that was just what it sounded like.

Okay, I thought, *there's no one actually around to tell right now. But if Mrs. Angotti knows, everyone will know soon enough.*

If we let her out of the house, Kai was doomed.

That was when I considered kidnapping as an option. And then I looked at everyone else's face and guessed that was what they were all thinking, too.

10

A Loud Noise

WHILE WE'D BEEN WORRYING ABOUT MRS. ANGOTTI, we hadn't been paying attention to Joey, who'd sneaked past us into the den and through the dining room, kitchen, and out the back door.

Robbie said, in a hushed voice that somehow got everyone's attention, "Where's Joey?"

"He was right here," Dr. Herks said, looking around.

Mrs. Angotti roared, "JOEY!!!"

And Martha raced toward the back door.

I was right behind her, and the others behind me, except for Robbie, of course.

By the time we got outside, there were four horse trailers lined up in neat rows, their loading doors open. They must have pulled in while we were with Mrs. Angotti, so stunned by her avalanche of words, we hadn't heard them arrive. But no one was anywhere in sight. The trucks' doors were wide open, and we could see clearly that no horses had been loaded. Yet.

"Where are they?" Martha grumbled.

"The barn!" I shouted.

By that time, Robbie had somehow managed to roll out of the door and down the ramp, but without anyone to push him, he couldn't get across the driveway. And the rest of us were so busy heading for the barn, we left him there. His voice followed us plaintively—"What about meeeeeee?"

We didn't bother to look anywhere but in the corridor of the barn where Agora and Kai were stabled. The blinds Dr. Herks had hung across the inside of the stall windows had all been yanked off. Some had landed inside the stall, and some, crumpled and stepped on, lay on the ground outside as riders and owners struggled to see through windows.

I could hear everyone muttering things like *abnormal, defective, bizarre.* None of them saw the magic, only the monstrous.

Suddenly, Joey's piercing voice cried out, "My mom calls it a FREAK OF NATURE!"

My hands bunched into fists.

Dr. Herks cleared a path to the stall by picking people up and moving them to one side, but in such a quick and gentle manner, no one had time or reason to complain.

I glanced into the stall. Ears back, teeth showing, Agora was straddling Kai. He was on his knees and sobbing uncontrollably for the first time since he'd been born, tears cascading down his face, his cheeks red with what could have been fever spots but were more likely fear. He'd never seen so many people before. So many loud, angry, scary people.

Her back to the door, Mom turned and shouted at everyone, those folks who had been our best boarders and who'd stayed longer and had been more loyal than the rest. She really unloaded on them.

"Move it, you big lump!" she cried to Mrs. Fischer, who is actually a *little* lump, smaller than me.

"*You're* the freaks," she said to the entire Proper family, who are usually just like their name.

"Get him out of there," she yelled, pointing at Joey.

Dr. Herks picked him up and set him to one side just like he was a bale of hay. A light bale of hay.

Martha's tongue practically sawed off limbs battling side by side with Mom. She even pushed Angela to the ground, which she hadn't done on purpose, but would have had she known then that it was Angela who'd brought everyone over to gape at Kai after Joey had shown him to her.

Angela began screaming as if she were about to be murdered. She has her mother's lungs, if not her vocabulary.

Me, I took the low route, crawling on my hands and knees till I got to the door. I had a set of keys on the lanyard around my neck, so I opened the door while everyone else was busy shouting and pushing and jostling for position. Then I crawled inside while Mom and Martha were doing their doubles act.

Agora knew me, so once I was in, the door shut firmly behind me, she made no angry move toward me.

I bent down and put my arms around Kai and sang into his ear, "*The eensy, weensy spider, went up the water spout.*" I tickled his nose until, like any toddler, he got distracted and began to smile.

Oddly, everyone outside began to cheer, and the noise set Agora off. She trotted to the door and bared her teeth again, pawing the ground as if getting ready to charge anyone who tried to get in.

But Kai seemed to think it was all part of a game. He clapped his hands and laughed, a fully human sound.

Or rather, he almost clapped them. It would be another day before he got that quite right.

The crowd stopped making loud noises, and Mrs. Proper said, "Isn't he *adorable?*" which seemed to come out of nowhere.

Wherever it came from, it worked. Everyone was all of a sudden agreeing and smiling, and maybe even *getting* it, except for Angela, who stomped off because there was nobody—not even her own mother—who wasn't cooing at the baby.

At which point Mom turned, and said in a controlled voice that probably only Martha and I recognized as her angry voice, "Come into the office, and I'll explain everything." And then in an undertone, she whispered through the window to me, "You stay here and keep the door locked." She started to go, then turned back. "No wait, first get your brother off the driveway."

Robbie—we'd all forgotten about Robbie!

Martha nodded at me before following the crowd to the office. "Gotta go help your mother feed the multitudes," she said. And when she saw the puzzled look on my face, she added, "Needing the dough and telling fish stories," which made less sense at first, since I knew they weren't going to be serving any food. Only after everyone was gone did I realize she was referring to the Bible story about the loaves and fishes and making puns at the same time.

It made me extra glad to be running off to get Robbie just to stay out of that crowd.

Games

THE OFFICE IS ACTUALLY THE FIRST TWO STALLS on the house side of the barn. Long before we'd come to live there, the former owner had renovated and insulated them. Now it's a comfortable workroom, heated in the winter, air-conditioned in the summer, with two deep, brown leather sofas and an armchair with a striped seat, where Mom can talk with boarders and visiting riders.

Mom changed none of the decorations or furniture when we took over. She said we'd better places to put our money, meaning—I think—into food for horses and new tack. Still, with a desk full of pictures—Mom and me, Robbie and me, Martha and me (though Martha's clearly snarling in the photo)—it looks like we put the room together ourselves. There's also a picture of me holding

Robbie when he first came home from the hospital. Pretty much all you can see is a bundle.

Any pictures of my dad were removed after he left. Mom may have thrown them away or put them in the burn barrel along with his jodhpurs and riding jeans. What she doesn't know is that I found a couple of pictures of him in an old album. I keep them in a box in my closet, along with his riding crop and the two blue ribbons he won on Bor at the county fair. I've never shown them to Robbie.

★ ★ ★

It was sure to be crowded in the office, what with the Angottis, Mr. and Mrs. Proper and their three children, Mrs. Fischer, and Professor Harries, who usually rode only on Sunday and was just here to collect her horse.

I turned and winked at Robbie. "Aren't we glad not to have to be official?" I said.

"It might be interesting," he said.

"It might be hot and full of angry people," I told him.

He nodded. "It might be full of Mrs. Angotti's words."

"And Joey picking his nose."

"And Angela sulking."

We ran out of *mights*, and I glanced over at Agora and Kai.

It would probably take some time before Agora could relax enough to let her ears come forward again. But Kai was already fine, lying down in the straw and playing with his fingers as if counting them.

I knelt down in the straw next to him and began to teach him a real game—peekaboo. After the first two times, he couldn't get enough of it, breaking out into peals of laughter every time my face appeared from behind my hands. I got tired of it long before he did.

Next I taught him patty-cake. And when I said, "Put it in the oven for Kai and me," he said, "Kai, Kai, Kai," and pointed to himself. So I taught him "Mama," for Agora, "Mom" for Mom, and "Marmar" for Martha, and of course "Robbie" and "Ari," though he had known some form of all those already. But this time we worked on proper pronunciation, no more baby talk.

Boy, was he quick!

Getting bored with the names and the patty-cake game—too tame, I suppose—he started back on peekaboo again, only this time getting to his feet and trotting over to play with Robbie, who had much more patience for the game than I did. They went on and on for such a long time, I walked over to Agora, who was getting anxious again because the two boys were laughing so loudly.

Brushing her mane almost did the trick. I could still see those little ripples of irritation running like rivers under her skin, but what finally soothed her was that Kai remembered that he was thirsty and came over to nurse.

Of course, as soon as he was done, he trotted back to Robbie. "More," he said.

"Should I tell him some nursery rhymes?" Robbie asked.

I nodded and he started on the horse rhymes he could remember, like "Ride a Cock Horse to Banbury Cross," "Trot, Trot to Boston," and "All the king's horses . . ."

Kai was standing by Robbie's chair and smiling and nodding his head to the rhythm of the rhymes when his eyes began to go half-mast. And between one recitation of "Humpty Dumpty" and the next, he fell asleep standing up.

"Wow," whispered Robbie, "isn't that *something*!"

"Just the way you used to fall asleep," I told him. "Milk and nursery rhymes and"—I snapped my fingers—"out you went."

He giggled. "I bet I didn't do it standing up!"

"You aren't a horse." I smiled at him. Neither one of us said that he couldn't stand by himself either. We didn't have to.

I turned to Agora. "He's all yours now."

She nickered, and her head bobbed as if saying, *Yes, he is.*

But he'd been hers from the very beginning. Unlike any of us humans, who looked at him funny, or who fainted when we saw him, or called him names like *freak* and *monster*, Agora had never shied away from Kai. Not once.

Nor—I thought fiercely—had Robbie.

So I left, checking Agora and Kai one last time before wheeling Robbie out of the stall and locking the door behind us. I peeked through the window, thinking that we needed to rehang those blinds. Not something I could do on my own.

Agora was nuzzling Kai, whose thumb and forefinger were both jammed into his mouth. He leaned against her as he slept but didn't wake up.

It had been a rough day for a young centaur.

☆ ☆ ☆

As Robbie and I got to the office, I was hit by the silence. I thought we'd missed the entire meeting, but I was wrong.

Pushing open the office door, I called, "Mom, listen . . ." Then I stopped.

What I'd thought was the quiet of an empty room was

anything but. It was filled with people silently scribbling down their thoughts. So without finishing my sentence, I pushed Robbie in.

They glanced up at us, heads swiveling in a single motion.

It seemed Mom had handed out paper and pens as a way of calming everyone down, asking them to write out suggestions about the best thing to do to keep a baby safe.

A *baby*.

Not a horse. Not a freak of nature. Not a monstrosity. A baby.

"Ari!" Joey cried out, waving his paper at me, our previous fight obviously forgotten.

Angela was not so forgiving. She sniffed—that sniff perfected with all the other high schoolers in town—and turned her back as if she'd more writing to do, but her pen never touched the paper again.

However, the rest of the folks in the office stared at me without a word.

They seemed to think I was the enemy.

Or the freak.

"Arianne, who's watching the foal?" Mom asked.

"His *mother*," I said. I hadn't meant it to come out quite that way, implying she should be watching out for Robbie and me, but there it was.

Mom got the pinch mark between her eyes, and Martha huffed through her nose at me. Dr. Herks shook his head, like I'd somehow disappointed him, and maybe I had. But someone had to say it.

"He's sleeping," I said.

Joey dropped his paper on the floor. "Can I go see?"

"No!" At least five voices answered him at the same time: Mom, Dr. Herks, Martha, me—and Mrs. Angotti, the last a surprise.

"I'll be quiet," Joey said and made a cross over his heart.

Mrs. Proper put her hand on his arm. "Joey, do you like people tiptoeing into your room when you're asleep?"

"If I was *asleep*, I wouldn't care, would I?"

But Mrs. Proper, in her quiet way, persisted. "But, Joey, what if you woke up and saw a stranger in your room?"

He gave a yelp. "I'd call the police!" He made it sound funny, but I could see in his eyes that he understood. At least he didn't ask again.

"In a nutshell, folks," Mom said, "*we* have to protect him. So let's read out those suggestions now."

Dr. Herks whispered to me, "She's bringing them all into the process. Helping them seek and possibly reach consensus, Quaker style."

I knew what he meant. Quakers don't make decisions

by majority rule. They keep talking about a problem until *everyone* agrees with the next step. It can take a *really* long time. But in the end, everyone is on board with the decision, and everyone feels that their objections have been fairly heard and fairly dealt with.

Dr. Herks stared at me. "You're frowning, Ari. What do *you* think?"

"I think it's *our* farm," I muttered, "and he's *our* centaur. And it's none of their business."

"But magic," Robbie whispered, "belongs to everybody, doesn't it?"

"Do you mean Kai is magic?" Dr. Herks asked.

Robbie thought about that for a minute, head cocked, jaw moving from side to side as if he was chewing on something.

Dr. Herks smiled and rubbed Robbie's head. "Well, *I* think that *all* birth is magic and all babies are magic as well."

Maybe, I thought. *But if he's not magic, then we've got* real *trouble.* Because all at once I remembered the stories about those nasty centaurs and the horrible things they did in ancient Greece. What if Kai turned out to be like them?

And then I thought, *Maybe Kai isn't magic after all, but some kind of miracle. Like the ones in the Bible. And the ones in the myths.*

Suggestions

As the suggestions were read out, I tried to hide my yawns. It wasn't just that I hadn't been sleeping well since Kai's birth. It was also that the suggestions were so predictable. In fact, they were the same ones we'd come up with ourselves.

The list went like this:

- *No gossiping about Kai.*
- *No talking to newspaper, radio, or TV reporters.*
- *No photographs of Kai or of Agora with him.*
- *No tattling in school or camp, not even to your best friend.* (That was Joey's idea.)
- *No writing in your diary about him.* (Angela's idea.)
- *No telling anyone who isn't here at the meeting, period!*

"Not even your husband?" Mrs. Angotti asked. "I gotta tell my *husband*. I mean he's my husband, after all, and we share everything, even stuff maybe we shouldn't share, but we do and—"

"I'm not telling mine," Mom said.

"That's different," Angela said disgustedly, "you're divorced. We don't believe in divorce."

Martha stood angrily and said, "This isn't about divorce. And it's sure not about writing in diaries. And don't anyone sing 'Kumbaya' now, or hold hands in a circle, or give me the kiss of peace." Then she walked out of the room.

Some folks looked puzzled, but I knew she was just trying to remind people to do what they'd promised.

Which wasn't much.

Mom shook everyone's hand and gave Professor Harries a hug because we knew her from our Quaker meeting. And then everyone left without taking a single horse away. In fact they scattered so quickly, it was as if no one was up for a ride or a lesson or even a visit with their horses. Which meant Martha and I would have a lot of extra work that afternoon. And Mom, too.

Again.

Joey and Angela and their mother were unusually quiet

as they walked toward their car, though Angela flicked a finger at the back of Joey's head when he started to speak. He pushed her in return. But for them, that was a moment of peace and calm.

After the trucks and cars had all pulled out—Mrs. Angotti's car spinning its wheels and throwing up gravel—Mom said to Dr. Herks, Robbie, and me, "I *believe* them." She bit her bottom lip before adding, "I *have* to believe them."

"Should I stay, Hannah?" His voice was soft and concerned.

She shook her head. "No, Gerry. You have to get your own work done. But call before dinner. In fact . . ." She hesitated, then said, "Come *for* dinner." She smiled at him.

He smiled back and nodded. "I'd like that."

They didn't touch hands or hug or do anything else except those smiles. But I had all my fingers crossed so hard behind my back, I almost sprained my right pinkie.

Oddly, Robbie took hold of my left hand. "It will work out, Ari," he whispered. "You'll see."

I didn't know if he meant Kai or if he meant Mom and Dr. Herks, or something else entirely.

"Maybe," I whispered back.

As Mom wheeled Robbie toward the house, Dr. Herks

turned to me. "Your mother is one of the world's true innocents, Arianne," he said. The furrows in his forehead were deeper than before, and his eyes blue-gray in the fading afternoon light.

"You don't believe they'll keep their silence," I said. It wasn't a question but a confirmation. And not a proper Quaker thought at all. We're supposed to look for the good in people. It's practically the only rule. "Well, *I* don't believe they will, either."

"Oh, I believe they were sincere when they promised," he said thoughtfully. "But having been a medic in a war zone, I have a different take on human nature than your mom. Even making a sincere promise won't stop a person from spilling the beans. It may happen by accident. Or someone may say something trying to impress a teacher or a boyfriend. Or whisper it as a secret to a trusted friend. Or maybe someone will *have* to tell their minister or rabbi. Or a husband or wife."

"Like Mrs. Angotti."

He nodded. "Someone might even talk in his or her sleep, or get angry at your mother if she raises her prices, or angry at Martha for . . . Well, God knows, I get angry at her often enough!"

"Me, too," I said. "But I love her."

"Of course you do." He nodded at me. "But however it happens, those beans are going to get spilled—it's the nature of beans, the nature of secrets. And that will end up hurting the little guy."

"Kai," I reminded him. "His name is Kai."

He nodded again, thoughtfully. "It'll hurt Hannah, too."

The way he said Mom's name was kind of prayerful. I don't remember Dad ever saying it that way.

"But something else is going on here, isn't it?" Dr. Herks looked at me searchingly. "Are you going to tell me, Arianne, or do I have to ask your mother?"

I stared at the ground unable to answer.

"It's not just about Kai," Dr. Herks said, trying to help.

I didn't want any help. I didn't want to go to that particular dark place.

But he was relentless, in that careful, caring Quaker way. "I don't want to pry, Arianne. But if this is getting in the way of our solving how to help Kai . . ."

And then without meaning to, it all flooded out of me. "When Robbie was born, he was called—well—a *seal boy*."

"I remember that in the papers. Thalidomide babies. People can be cruel to the unusual."

I nodded, never taking my eyes off the ground. "The

doctors weren't sure he'd ever learn to walk. Or talk. Or turn over in his crib. He was one big birth defect."

"That's a *horrible* way to put it, Arianne. I'm surprised at you."

I took a big breath. "That's not *me* speaking. I loved Robbie from the very first. Mom did, too. We took turns holding him and feeding him. My dad was the one who said that about him, called him a monster. And then he left us." I guess I was wondering if Dr. Herks would leave, too. Or that all the attention to Kai might bring unwanted attention to Robbie. Or that both boys would get called *monsters*. And a dozen other things besides.

This time Dr. Herks looked down at the ground, and those blue eyes turned the color of steel. "I see," he said and was silent.

I believe he did see, but the silence grew between us.

At last I said, "So what are we going to do?"

"I'm not entirely sure." He put a hand on my shoulder. "But know this, Ari—you and Robbie and Kai mean a lot to me."

"And Mom?"

"A lot more than you know. So if you need me, call, and I'll be back like a shot, guns blazing."

It wasn't a very Quakerly thing to say, more a Vet thing.

Which was okay by me. Then he held out his hand, and I shook it, just like soldiers do before a big battle. At least that's what they do in the movies.

✯ ✯ ✯

After dinner and all the excitement and worry and hard work of the day, I fell asleep in front of the television in the middle of Mom's favorite show, *Mister Ed*. She sure loved that talking horse. Laughed even when it wasn't funny, sometimes saying things like, "I swear that if Bor could talk, he'd sound like that!"

She woke me and sent me up to bed.

"I'd have carried you upstairs if you were still small," she said, her eyes suddenly pooling.

"Mom?" I wondered what she was crying about—all the tension of the day, the memory of me as a child, long before anything bad had happened to our family . . .

She wiped a hand across her face, and her eyes were clear.

"Dr. Herks?" I mumbled.

She shook her head. "Emergency surgery on a pony hit by a car." She shrugged. "He'll be over later if he can. To check on Kai."

I nodded, thinking, *And check on us, too.* And then I went up to bed, where I dreamed about geese flying over the farm, and each one had the head of my dad on its shoulders. Down below, armed with a rifle, Dr. Herks was getting ready to shoot. In the dream, I was shouting at him. When I woke, I didn't know if I'd wanted Dr. Herks to shoot or was trying to stop him.

13

Lull Before the Storm

WE HAD A WONDERFUL WEEK AFTER THAT. Kai might have been only twenty-eight days old, and while still clearly a foal from the waist down, his human part already looked six or seven. He seemed to become less horselike every day, spending time with Agora when he needed to nurse or sleep, but when Robbie or I were around, always paying attention to us, our words, our gestures, the way we laughed.

Martha had given him some of her rubber bands to tie his hair back with. He preferred the blue ones. And she'd taught him how to make the ponytail himself.

Ponytail! We all had a good giggle about that. Even Kai.

He was playing a lot with Robbie every day, imitating Robbie's speech, listening hard as Robbie read him books. And he was starting to read himself, though he didn't like the baby picture books, preferring history and stories about myths—Greek and Roman and Viking were his favorites.

He went back to Agora only when he napped or when he wanted to nurse. If Agora was worried or unhappy or upset with him, she didn't show it.

Early on, Dr. Herks had pointed out that Kai was having a growth spurt. "As if the boy Kai has to keep up with the horse Kai."

In fact, boy Kai had gone from infant to toddler in the first couple of days, and then from toddler to something like a three-year-old by the end of the week. He got all his baby teeth, then lost his first and then his second. When I tried to explain the tooth fairy, he had just giggled and said, "Not true!" As if only he was magic and he couldn't believe anyone else was. I wondered what would happen when we got to Santa Claus or the Bible.

Meanwhile, his hair was growing in thick and shaggy like a mane, with an odd waviness once the curls had grown out. His large eyes always seemed to be searching for something new to do. And he repeated absolutely everything anyone said in a voice that Mom called *flutelike*, meaning—I think—it was high-pitched and full of music.

His vocabulary grew quickly. During his first few days, he had added words like *doh* for the stall door and *dink* for wanting a drink—whether water or milk. He rubbed his eyes, repeating *seep, seep, seep* when he was tired and needed to nap.

I was "Ari," Robbie was "Brob," and Dr. Herks "Dada."

But by the end of that week, he was already talking in short sentences—"Kai wants more" and "No, don't want to" were favorites. And "Ari, gimme." The start of the second week, he was speaking in longer sentences, and in between, there were whinnies and snorts, which he directed at Agora. Occasionally he spoke to Martha that way, since she clearly understood Horse. So by the third week, we were all having actual conversations.

Sometimes I'd just go into the stall and read aloud to Robbie and Kai. I was really into my new favorite book, *A Wrinkle in Time*, and Robbie had decided that he wanted to be called Charles Wallace and eat bread and jam for breakfast the entire week. Kai tried to copy him, but he spit out the jam until Mom gave him apple butter on his bread. After that, he couldn't get enough.

Kai didn't understand much about the story, of course. He might have been growing fast, but he wasn't ready for science fiction. Still, he loved hearing the words, and he repeated *tesseract* over and over, as if it had some kind of meaning that none of us could understand.

Robbie made up a little song that he taught Kai:

Tesseract folds the space,
Keeps the magic in its place.
Tesseract holds the key
To a father's memory.

Ali, Ali, home free.
Ali, Ali, home free.
Ali, Ali, home free,
We all fall down.

Each time Robbie sang the word *tesseract*, Kai would shout it out in his high-pitched voice and then giggle through the next line of the song. It kept them entertained for hours.

I could only stand the song about five times through before I had to close the book and leave. Sometimes I took Agora out with me. She always seemed happy to go as well. I'd let her run around the paddock for a bit, and she kicked her heels up like a colt, all that old arthritis strangely gone. More magic, I suppose.

☆ ☆ ☆

In the fourth week, a few of our riders came to work their horses or to help out in the barn, but most of the time we had the farm to ourselves. It was grand, even with the extra work, because it seemed as if the worst of our worries about Kai were over. The people at the farm were the ones who knew about Kai, but they were keeping it quiet. We became a family and not just a business with a secret at its heart.

Mom seemed more relaxed since . . . well, since I couldn't remember when. She even started baking again, cupcakes and angel food cake (my favorite) and a honey cake that proved to be the one Kai liked best. He could eat an entire cake by himself. Well, a small cake, anyway.

☆ ☆ ☆

Once during that fourth week, on a break from the two boys, I went to help Martha with Professor Harries' gelding. He's not neat at either end.

"Isn't the farm wonderful, this quiet?" I said as I mucked out my side of the stall.

"Lull before the storm," Martha replied tartly, a blue rubber band holding her hair straight back. She said the words as if she was biting each one in half, so I didn't dare ask her what she meant.

Later, I found Mom with Bor and asked her to explain what Martha said.

"Martha's a pessimist, and I'm an optimist."

"*Mom!*"

She gave an exaggerated shrug. "Martha is sure this peace—the lull—won't hold and that someone will tell, and *that* will put us in the middle of the biggest storm ever."

"Dr. Herks thinks so, too."

"Well, I have more faith in people than that. Martha's faith is only in horses. They're simpler. It's an easy choice."

"And Dr. Herks?"

She turned back to Bor and held her hand out, and he nuzzled her palm contentedly, never pulling his lips back, just his hot breath sending her warm love. "Gerry saw a lot of awful stuff in 'Nam, and he's dealing with it slowly." Her voice was soft. "But he *is* dealing with it."

It turned out that Mom was right for the entire week and a bit more. And Martha was right afterward. But for that time before the storm, Robbie and I spent hours and hours in Agora's stall. With how quickly Kai was growing, we didn't want to miss *anything*.

By the end of the week, Dr. Herks had set up a run for Kai by blocking both ends of the corridor outside Agora's stall, saying, "He needs the exercise."

It turned out Kai had an absolute passion for speed, all his little hooves sometimes lifting off the floor at the same time. But because both ends of the corridor were blocked off, gated and locked, he couldn't run away.

Kai wants to gallop, he would beg when he wanted to go out, and as soon as he was let loose in the corridor, he raced up and down, incredibly pleased with himself and screaming in delight.

Agora would walk sedately behind him. Of course she couldn't keep up. Well, who could? But whenever Kai became too boisterous, her whinny always brought him galloping back to her side.

"I wish I'd been able to discipline you two that way," Mom said that first morning we watched Kai and Agora in their run.

"*Mom!*" Robbie and I said together.

She put out her hands to us, and we each took one.

"Love you, too, Mom," I whispered.

"Me three," said Robbie, and sang out:

> *Me three,*
> *We three,*
> *That makes*
> *A family!*

"It sure does," said Mom.

"And there's Kai, too," Robbie said. "Or Kai four."

"And Martha," Mom reminded him. "So five."

I almost added Dr. Herks' name then, but instead bit my lip to keep myself from jinxing that dream.

Later, watching Kai sleeping in the stall, Dr. Herks remarked, "I think he's only got an on and off switch, nothing in between."

That made Mom laugh so loud, she snorted. Then Dr. Herks started laughing as well, as if he'd caught the laugh flu. Soon the two of them were like little kids, snorting and giggling and unable to stop.

"Cut it out, you two," I said.

Robbie added, "You're gonna wake the baby."

That started them laughing all over again, and I had to shove them out of the stall as if I was the mother and they the naughty children.

✹ ✹ ✹

Besides cake and apple butter on toast, Kai adored apples and carrots, though we had to cut them into small pieces because he didn't yet have all of his permanent teeth.

"And because we don't want him choking," Dr. Herks said.

Kai also loved peanut butter and bolted down oatmeal in the mornings as long as there was plenty of raw milk and cooked McIntosh apples mixed in.

Dr. Herks warned us we had to keep him on a vegetarian diet. "We've no idea if his body can process meat products," he said. "Horses don't eat meat." Then he mused, "Maybe if he has two stomachs the way he has two hearts . . ."

However, without actually x-raying Kai, we couldn't be sure, and we weren't about to get him an X-ray because then his "oddness" would be revealed.

So we kept the secret and the lull that went with it. We thought it was for Kai's sake, but a good part was for our own sakes as well.

※ ※ ※

The first sign of the oncoming storm was a phone call from Mrs. Angotti. I picked up the receiver in the living-room phone the same time Mom picked up the one in the kitchen.

"I'm sorry, so very sorry, because I didn't want this to happen and I promise you she'll be punished for letting it out, but Angela told her best friend, Zoe, who swore she'd say nothing, but you know teenagers and she had a fight with Angela over something, which if I ever find out what it is, heads will roll or at least bounce a bit, but they're friends again so it's no use following that particular trail!"

Clearly Mrs. A had lost her ability to punctuate in her rush to get everything said, I thought. She continued in that same breathless manner: "Because of that fight, she wrote something for a paper in her summer psychology class, I mean Zoe, not Angela, who doesn't take psychology but physics in summer school, but where she gets the brains for that, it's not from me or her father, I'll tell you, neither one of us can balance a checkbook. You see, her father has an accountant do that for him in his business, that is, not at home." She finally took a breath.

Mom said quickly, "What did she say?"

"Who?" It was the shortest sentence I ever heard Mrs. Angotti utter, which just goes to show how sorry she was.

"Zoe."

"Zoe didn't say anything, she *wrote* it, in her paper like I told you, which the teacher said was the best essay in the summer class even if it was only science fiction, and she sent it to the *Boston Herald*'s kids' writing contest and—"

Mom said again, "What did Zoe *say* in the essay?"

Mrs. Angotti took a *big* breath this time, as if getting a hurricane's worth of wind. "She said that a friend of a friend had a horse farm where a centaur was born that was half child and half horse, and then went into a full analysis of the kind of emotional problems such a child would face, calling it *liminality*. I had to look up the word and I still don't get it but evidently Zoe says it's the very latest thing in brain work, whatever that is."

Mom interrupted her, "Science fiction? Space walks? *Twilight Zone? John Carter of Mars?* Then that's okay. Nobody really believes that stuff."

I hung up carefully. I knew it *wasn't* okay. I ran into the kitchen just as Mom was putting the phone back on its stand.

"What should we do?"

She looked up, startled. "Why, nothing, my little eavesdropper. Stay off the phone when I'm on it. That way you won't hear silly talk from Mrs. Angotti. And stop worry-ing. Nobody in his right mind will believe for a minute what that girl wrote. She said it was science *fiction*!"

Kai, at least, was real.

Very real.

But I knew it wouldn't be long till we had people lining up outside our barn door for a glimpse of him. And when they came, the reporters wouldn't be far behind.

14

Under Siege

THE VERY NEXT MORNING, even before I got downstairs for breakfast, the phone rang. After the third ring, Mom picked it up.

I could hear her shouting into the phone, saying, "Yes, yes, no—and where'd you get that . . . well, it's wrong. Don't you understand these two words? *Science. Fiction.* Yes, science fiction. Little green men. *Forbidden Planet. The Twilight Zone.* No!" And she slammed the phone down so hard, it made me wince.

"That's nine words, Mom," I said as I walked into the kitchen. "Or maybe eleven."

The phone began ringing again. Mom stared at it as if it were a rabid dog getting ready to bite her. Then she turned and went into the bathroom without saying a word. I could hear the water running, and I figured she was throwing cold water on her face, so I sat down at the table and grabbed a blueberry muffin, ignoring the phone until the Ansafone, our brand-new answering machine, picked it up.

An accusing voice left a simple message. "Nobody hangs up on me, lady."

The phone rang twice more.

"Don't answer it," Mom called out.

The minute a fourth call came in, I waited till the caller hung up, then picked up the receiver and phoned Martha and then Dr. Herks.

Mom came back into the kitchen, two red spots on her cheeks as if she'd scrubbed away tears.

Five minutes later—a long five minutes—Martha showed up in her bathrobe and boots, hair pulled back in two green rubber bands. Dr. Herks arrived soon after.

Mom pointed at the phone and said one word. "Monsters."

As if encouraged by that, the phone rang again.

"Don't answer it," I said.

But the phone was already in Martha's hand. She listened for a minute, said, "Horse pucky!" and hung up.

"That's not going to slow them down at all," Dr. Herks said. "Time for Plan B."

But we didn't have a Plan B. We didn't even have a Plan A.

"I'll watch at the barn," Martha said.

"Get some proper barn gear on first," Mom told her. "If . . ." She took a deep breath, then let it out slowly. "*If* there are photographers . . ."

Martha got a hard look on her face and pinched lines all around her eyes. "It's not like I'm any kind of a model," she said, shrugging, but she went back to her house to get dressed.

"I'll guard the barn till Martha gets there," I said.

"No, Arianne, I will." Dr. Herks squared his shoulders. "I've got a parade-ground voice and a hard hand."

I wasn't sure what he meant, but nodded.

"Your mother needs you here," he added unnecessarily, and was gone.

☆ ☆ ☆

The phone rang five more times, and Mom answered them all in case they were our riders. Mostly she spoke in monosyllables—"Yes. No. No. Yes"—slamming the phone down each time until I was worried she was going to break it.

I went into Robbie's room to get him up and dressed, if necessary, but he'd already managed it himself. He does that most days. It always takes him longer than it would if I dressed him, but Mom says that it's important to let him do it because it builds confidence. I didn't believe that for a long time, but now I know she's right.

When we returned, Mom had the phone in her hand and was clutching it so hard, her knuckles had gone white. I wondered if it was the Monster again.

"Golly, Mom, are you okay?" Robbie asked. I pushed him over to her, and he grabbed her free hand.

Just then, Dr. Herks came back in, saying, "Martha's holding the fort. She's got a shovel and pitchfork by her side. She even scares *me* and—" Then he saw how stricken Mom looked and how white Robbie's face was. Taking the phone from Mom, he hung it up.

"No one says you have to answer, Hannah. But if you find it impossible not to let the phone just ring, we can take it off the hook."

"Thank you, Gerry." Her voice was shaky, low. She looked up at the ceiling, as if catching his eye was the last thing she wanted to do. She talked to the ceiling, too. "I'll be okay in a minute. We need the phone. This *is* a business after all. But you see, everybody promised not to . . . science . . . fiction . . . essay . . . *Boston Herald* . . . confirmed sources . . ." And then she began to cry softly.

Robbie had never seen her cry before, and he started whimpering. I pulled him over to me. "Not to worry, Squinch. Just someone stupid on the phone hurt her feelings."

"I *hate* stupid!" he said. And then sang a couple of lines of a made-up song to the tune of "Yankee Doodle."

> *Stupid people called the house,*
> *Early in the morning*
> *Made my mother really cry . . .*

"Oh, Ari," he whined, "I can't think of a rhyme for *morning.*"

It was hard to tell if he was more upset about the rhyme or Mom, but I said, "Borning, corning, horning, scorning, warning—"

"Aha!" He smiled his glorious smile, the upset forgotten. "*Warning!* Thanks, Ari."

Meanwhile, Dr. Herks had put his arms around Mom and said into her hair, "It will be all right, dear girl."

My eyes got big. I felt my heart skip a beat.

Robbie sang, "*So listen, here's my warning.* Is that good, Ari?"

I didn't answer. Robbie would figure it out on his own. He always did. Instead, I turned to Dr. Herks, ignoring the fact that he was hugging Mom, and summed up what I'd heard Mrs. Angotti say about the summer psychology class and Zoe's teacher sending the essay to the *Boston Herald.*

Wiping her eyes with a tea towel, Mom added, "The reporter said he confirmed the sighting with two sources."

"Wanna bet it's Joey and Angela?" I said.

"And so it starts," Dr. Herks muttered.

"You were right," Mom said between snuffles and into the front of his jacket.

"I hate being right."

"They meant the promise when they said it," I reminded her.

She nodded more to Dr. Herks than to me. "Lack of sleep does *not* help." She pulled away from him. "Let's go give Martha a hand."

"Robbie," I said, "you stay here. Man the phone."

"No way," Robbie said. "I'm not a man, and I want to take care of my brother."

"Brother?" Dr. Herks asked.

"It's what he calls Kai."

Martha was no longer standing quietly with the pitchfork by her side. Now it was in her hand, the sharp tines pointing at the throat of a disheveled-looking redheaded man who was backed up against the barn. His arms were raised, maybe in prayer, and his face was bone white. There were large, untidy damp patches under his arms, staining his blue-striped shirt. He must have arrived around the time Dr. Herks and I were comforting Mom. His camera lay at his feet on the concrete floor of the barn's corridor. It was small and black with the word NIKON on its front.

"Please, lady . . . ," he was saying, his voice high-pitched, shaking.

"Martha," Dr. Herks used what must have been his soldier voice, "put . . . the . . . pitchfork . . . down."

She didn't turn around or lower the pitchfork, but said in her own version of the voice, "He's a dang *pappanazzi* taking pictures of things he isn't meant to see. He's on land he wasn't invited to. And he's threatened me and mine. His kind killed Marilyn Monroe, hounding her everywhere she went, poor kid, and I won't have him here on the farm."

I said to Dr. Herks, "Who's Marilyn Monroe?"

Mom answered, "A movie star."

"Did a pappanazzi actually kill her?"

"I think she means *paparazzo*," Mom said. "Martha reads too many movie magazines."

Robbie piped up, "What's a paparazzo?"

"They call themselves photojournalists and track down celebrities, movie stars, and rock-and-roll singers," Dr. Herks said. "Then they take pictures of them, which they sell to magazines."

I whispered to Mom, "Maybe Dr. Herks reads those magazines, too."

"But," Robbie whispered to me, "Kai's no celebrity."

As soon as he said that, my traitor mind added, *Yet*.

"Hey," begged the photographer, "can you call the crazy lady off?"

Dr. Herks put out a hand to either side, as a warning to Mom, Robbie, and me to stay right where we were. Then he walked to where Martha stood and glared at the red-headed man.

"My name is Gerald Arthur Herks. I am the veterinarian for this farm. I am also a captain in the army. Who and what are you?"

In a shaky voice, the redheaded man said, "I'm a

freelance photographer, sir." He straightened his shoulders a bit. "An award-winning photographer. Name is Nathan Fern. Sent to town to get a picture of a local contest winner, Zoe Krosoczka. She told me her story was about something real that happened on this farm. And even though I thought it preposterous, it always pays to check. So I thought . . . well . . . you know . . . came over. And I got attacked by the harpy with the fork! Here's my identity card." His fingers shook as he fumbled in his shirt pocket and drew out two very crushed and dirty cards.

Dr. Herks took the cards, glanced at them, tucked the cleanest one into his shirt pocket, then said, "Well, Nathan, here's what we're going to do," in a voice that was low and controlled. "*You* are going to give me your camera, and I'm going to dump any pictures you made of our farm. If you ever come onto our property again without an invitation, I'll call the police and confiscate the camera. Then I will sue you within an inch of your life, as you will be in violation of law 1-7-1-9 of the penal code. Oh, and the next time, I won't stop Martha here from sticking her pitchfork into you as far as she can reach. Are we clear?"

"Clear . . . um . . . sir."

"Good," said Dr. Herks. He took the camera, opened it, and unspooled the film before turning to Martha and saying in a more genial voice, "Put the pitchfork down now, Martha."

"Are you sure, Captain, sir?" She snapped out the *sir* like a soldier.

He nodded. "I'm sure."

Only then did she do as he said, but slowly.

After that, Dr. Herks handed the camera back to Nathan Fern, who grabbed it and ran to his car. He got in and left so fast, his tires carved a long strip in our gravel drive.

"Wow!" said Robbie, gazing up at Dr. Herks with awe on his face.

As soon as Fern was out of there, Dr. Herks, Mom, and Martha burst out laughing. Dr. Herks wiped his mouth with the back of his sleeve.

"What's law 1-7-1-9 of the penal code?" I asked.

"Oh, Arianne," Dr. Herks said, still laughing, "your mom will say I'm a terrible model for you and Robbie!"

I looked at him strangely.

"I lied."

"You *lied*?" Robbie asked. "Cool!"

"I made it up."

"He *made it up*!" I said, and then I was laughing with the rest of them. A moment later, Robbie was laughing as well.

15

A Night with Kai

THE DAY WENT ALONG slowly and quietly after that. I did all my before-dinner chores and came back into the house to find that Dr. Herks had been invited to dinner once again and this time had brought along two large pepperoni pizzas he'd made himself.

"My specialty," he said. "Mother was first-generation Italian, Father was Greek. I got the Greek looks and the Italian food genes."

"Either way works for me," Mom said in a dreamy sort of way that made me smile.

We made a salad and some garlic bread. Martha brought wine for the grown-ups. Robbie and I had milk, mine white, his chocolate.

As much as we tried to make it a festive time, dinner was tense. We ate and talked and ate some more.

We talked about everything *but* Kai: How the apple order had to be doubled, whether new fences should be built, whether a separate barn needed to be put up, and how much it might cost. In a way, though, everything we said was really about Kai. More apples was a Kai thing, the separate barn would be for him, new fences—again Kai.

Halfway between the last piece of pizza and ice cream for dessert, Dr. Herks' pager went off and he phoned his office. "I've got a difficult situation here at Hannah's farm," he said. "It's tricky, but nothing catching. Please direct all emergency calls to Dr. Small." He didn't mention Kai.

Yes, I was eavesdropping. And no, I didn't feel guilty about it. It was, as Dr. Herks said, *a difficult situation*.

✫ ✫ ✫

Something else wasn't said. Evidently a Plan B had been made without anyone telling Robbie or me. Mom and Dr. Herks and Martha had decided it while I was out doing my chores and Robbie was in his room watching television.

Plan B consisted of Martha sleeping the first part of

the night on the couch in the barn office and Dr. Herks sleeping downstairs on the sofa in the living room. Then at midnight or one A.M., they'd change. He'd go out to the barn, and Martha would go to bed in her own little house.

And Mom? She was to get a good night's sleep in her own bed this time.

This time. That sounded ominous. And I only found this out when everyone started to settle in for the night.

I hadn't even been considered as the one to sleep near Kai. So I raised my hand like I have to in school and said, "I could—"

Robbie added, "We could do it *together.*"

The adults interrupted in chorus: "Absolutely not."

Mom added, "This needs a grown-up, kids."

"I'm grown up enough to feed and exercise the horses," I pointed out. "I'm grown up enough to clean out stalls. I'm old enough to be trusted with the biggest secret ever."

Robbie didn't say a word.

"There's no danger in any of that," Mom said, her voice low, careful, but she looked over at Dr. Herks as she said it.

I didn't ask what danger. The memory of Martha and the pitchfork was sharp enough.

I stayed up as late as I could, but Robbie went quietly into his own room and didn't even turn on his TV. He must have been asleep before nine. Mom, too, didn't make it past nine, retiring to her room after a long, hot bath.

I managed to stay up until ten, still hoping to be included in the grown-up end of things, but a little after the grandfather clock chimed the hour, I was yawning hard, so Dr. Herks sent me to bed. I'm ashamed to say that I fell right to sleep.

My old room had been the quiet room, away from road noise, not that there's much of it. We're the last farm on the paved road. After us, there's nothing but a bumpy gravel path for about a hundred yards, and then forest land for miles. Our farm owns about ten acres of the forest, and the rest belongs to the government.

In the winter, loads of Ski-Dooers go roaring down the road and through the woods. Although Martha had threatened to set out chain-link fences strategically on the trails near our farm, Mom wouldn't let her because she liked to keep the trails open for anyone who uses them responsibly. Of course, every time a snowmobiler roars past our house in the dead of winter, Martha says, "Nothing responsible about that!"

When Robbie was born, Mom switched me to the bigger room, the one with windows looking out over the road. The only noisy bedroom in the house.

I liked being away from everyone else. And I hardly ever woke up when something noisy drove by.

However, the whole Kai thing made me sleep lightly that night, which is why I woke up at one A.M. precisely. Something was driving slowly up and down our road. As it went along, I heard our grandfather clock ring its single chime, so I knew what time it was.

I sat up in the dark and watched out the window as a car crept past the farm, got as far as the gravel road—I could hear how the road sounds changed—and then it turned around. When it kept on past us, going back toward the Suss farm, I let out the breath I hadn't known I was holding.

Pulling on my jeans, I tucked my nightgown into them, put on my sneakers, and placed the lanyard with the barn keys around my neck. Then I grabbed a flashlight and tiptoed down the stairs.

I didn't wake Mom because Dr. Herks had said she needed her sleep. I figured I'd just go and check to be sure no one had gotten out of the car. If I saw or heard even the smallest thing, I'd tell whoever was asleep in the barn. I wasn't planning to be a hero or anything. I wasn't stupid.

Maybe it wasn't Plan B, since I'd had no part of that. Maybe it was Plan C, which was all my own.

I carried a flashlight for its light as well as a possible weapon. Night had tucked in over the barn, but I wasn't fooled into thinking it would be like a cozy blanket. Mom told me that the horses always watch you in the dark with the attention of any wild animal, waiting for what will happen next, ready to flee if they don't like what they see. As they are in stalls, they can't flee very far, but the possibility is there, a kind of electricity in the air, their eyes shifting, even if nothing else moves.

Being in the barn in the middle of the night is very different from being there in the daylight. I'd never been out here so late except for the time Mom and Robbie and I went to see the Perseids, and the time we went for a Christmas night sleigh ride at the Suss farm pulled by their two heavy horses. But those were early nights compared to this.

I expected it to be spooky outside, but there was an almost-full moon, which lit everything enough so I didn't even need the flashlight. Still, I kept it ready, in case there really *was* someone sneaking around.

Someone besides me, that is.

I sure didn't want to trip over a bucket or a bridle once

I was inside, because I didn't want to scare off any intruders before I could identify them.

It was past time for insects to be flying, or bats. Maybe even past owl time. At least I didn't see any of them, or hear them call. The horses in the front barn were all quiet, probably asleep. After checking on them, I swung around to the other side of the barn to see if anyone was near Agora's stall. Taking the keys from around my neck, I opened the stall door. It creaked so loudly, I expected Martha or Dr. Herks to come galloping over, pitchfork in hand.

That's when I heard snoring from the office. It was loud, stuttering, a long, drawn-out sound. An army could have marched in here and taken Kai away, and we wouldn't have known.

So much for Plan B!

As I got inside, I turned on my flashlight, since the moon couldn't penetrate into the stall, especially with the blinds back over the windows and door.

Agora looked up sleepily.

"Just me, girl," I said.

Comforted, she lay back down. But her movement must have awakened Kai, because he clambered up on his knobby legs and began to charge toward me.

"Whoa, there!" I said, holding out my arms to keep him from knocking me over in his excitement.

He held out his arms too, just a little kid wanting a hug. A little kid with four legs. He smelled of both talc and horse. Martha must have given him a good scrub before he went to sleep, powdering his back and under his arms and on what she called the "seam lines" where his boy body met the horse. She'd shown me how there was sometimes a bit of irritation there, the rough horse hair rubbing against the little boy's much more delicate skin.

"Good Kai," I whispered.

"Good Ari," he whispered back.

I giggled and put my face down into his mane.

"Go out now?" he asked. "Kai can go out and run?"

"No, Kai," I said. "It's dark out there."

"Dark in here," he said matter-of-factly. "I see in the dark."

Like a horse, I thought.

The car I'd heard earlier was long gone—probably just stupid teenagers out joyriding, though it hadn't sounded very full of joy. But that's what Martha calls it anyway. There seemed to be no one else around for miles. At least no one awake.

"Okay, but you have to stay close and listen to me. And

when I say it's time to come back in, you have to come. I can't go chasing after you. Not in the dark. *I* can't see in the dark."

"Okay, Ari," he said. "I'm sorry."

I nodded. "Promise?"

"Prrrrrromise!" His voice was breathily positive, as if he actually knew what a promise was.

I picked up one of my old sweaters that was hanging on the door and wrestled it over him. It was too big for him, so I had to help him with the sleeves. He giggled as I rolled them up.

"Don't want you getting cold out there," I said. Actually, it was a soft August night, and Kai seemed as resistant to mild night temperatures as the rest of the horses.

"What is *cold*, Ari?" he asked.

I put my arms around him and made a shiver and said, "Brrrrr."

He giggled and repeated the sound. But I wasn't sure he got it.

"Cold wind," I said. "Ice and snow. Freeze. Low temperature."

"I've read about snow," he said. "When can I see it?"

"Not for months," I told him. "But it's really cold."

"Brrrr," he said, and grinned.

"Never mind," I said, and took his warm little hand in mine. "There's plenty of time for snow." We went out into the corridor, and he began to run before I had a chance to lock the door into the paddock. He cantered down to where the door stood ajar and then ran right into the paddock with the kind of knock-kneed joy that all colts have. In a moment, he had gone into the darkness near the trees.

I ran after him, calling in a desperate whisper, "Kai, get back here, now!"

Hera put her nose out of her stall, top female protecting her herd. She whickered quietly, and Kai trotted back to whinny at her. His voice sounded much more human than horse.

And then I thought, *Come on, Ari, it's night. Daylight is the problem, not the dark. No one can see him now, but he can see in the dark. Let him run around a little bit without yammering at him. Maybe that's part of Plan C!* I touched the horse part of his back. "Okay, Kai—go run in the paddock. But come back the moment I call!"

Off he went, outlined by moonlight, out where Mom and Robbie and I had watched the star shower last year, a time when life was predictable, if not always happy. A time when I'd wanted magic to come into my life. Before I wondered if that was what I really wanted after all.

He stopped in the grass and turned to me. "Soft," he said.

"Grass," I told him.

He spread his front legs wide and bent over until he could touch the tops of the grass, then pulled some up and sniffed at it.

"What does it smell like?"

He giggled. "Grass." He rose on his hind feet and flung his arms wide. "It smells like *grass*, Ari!"

"Shush," I cautioned, but I was too late, for he was suddenly running around the field close to the fence. The moon outlined his body, and he seemed to glow, like something out of a legend—otherworldly, beautiful. Something too wonderful to be kept hidden in a small, square, concrete-floored stall.

Magic! This time I was certain of it. *Magic should never be contained*, I thought. *It should run free in this world.* I was smiling so broadly my lips began to ache, and I didn't care a bit.

Stopping, Kai leaned down and plucked some of the long grass near the fence and put it in his mouth.

He spit it right out. "Poo, Ari," he said, immediately trying another handful, but spitting it out as well. "No, no, no!" His voice rose, like a two-year-old having a tantrum. "No, no, no!"

I put my finger to my lips. "Shhhhh," I said, "or we'll have to go back inside."

He mimicked me and held his finger up, touching his lip. And as he did, something flashed.

I looked up at the sky.

No stars falling, though a lot of them glared down at us.

The flash came again. This time from beyond the fence.

Then another. And another.

I spun around, screamed, "Run, Kai, run back to the barn! Run! Run! Run!"

16

Lemons

Kai must have heard the terror in my voice, because he immediately galloped away, heading for the safety of his stall, his hair and mane flagging out behind as he ran.

Once he was in the barn, I could hear his feet scrabbling on the concrete floor and was afraid he was going to fall and break a leg. A horse with a broken leg is a doomed creature. If the horse can't stand on the leg, then he can't maintain normal blood pressure. Death is only a matter of time. That's why a vet will put down a horse with a badly broken leg—so as not to prolong its suffering.

I tried not to imagine it. Gasping in fear, I followed Kai into the barn, making enough noise to wake up anyone.

But it was far too late to worry about that.

The flashes behind us had come in steady succession, like July Fourth fireworks.

Then someone on the Suss side of the fence had called out, "Run here, Kai, come here, Kai." Then the voice cried, "Look at the birdie, Kai!"

But thankfully, Kai was already gone.

And I wasn't far behind.

☆ ☆ ☆

By the time Kai was in his stall, the house and barn lights were blazing. Martha was there with her pitchfork, her nightgown flapping about her boots. Mom had taken up guard duty in front of Kai's stall, holding on to a rolling pin I didn't even know we owned.

Hair standing up in sleep-spikes, Dr. Herks was already by the fence, glaring into the darkness. He had a pistol in his hand.

"We're calling the police," he shouted. "In the meantime, I'm armed. And as a captain in the army, I have a gun permit. Trust me, I know how to shoot!"

A pistol!

A threat of violence!

Try explaining *that* in our Quaker meeting. We're all supposed to be pacifists, a fancy grown-up way of saying we're against war in all its forms and against weapons entirely. But Dr. Herks had been a soldier before he was a Quaker.

There was a sudden flurry on the other side of the fence, a car door slammed. Tires squealed out of the field.

Behind me our horses were kicking at the stall doors, whinnying their distress. Bor was bugling, Hera practically screaming.

As for Agora, she'd backed Kai up against the far wall of their stall and pushed him down so she could stand over him. Her lips were drawn back over her yellowed teeth. No one—not even me—was going to get near him again this night.

Beneath her, Kai was sobbing as if his heart was breaking.

And maybe it was.

☆ ☆ ☆

It was all my fault. I was the one who had taken him out, who encouraged him to run about in the open field—the one who'd let him be exposed. There was no wriggle room in my conscience to explain away my guilt.

"Sooner or later, we were gonna have to face it," Martha said. "And as I'd fallen asleep on watch, this was really *my* fault, Ari, not yours."

Arms around me, Mom said, "It was bound to happen, honey."

"But this was too *soon*," I mumbled into Mom's arms. "Kai wasn't ready. *We* weren't ready."

Pacing back and forth and thinking out loud, Dr. Herks said, "It must have been that Fern guy. So, how good are his photos? If he was rushed, frightened, maybe not so good. And it's night. Night-vision cameras are mostly army stuff. Not really in public use. And used for spying, not taking pictures. With a regular camera the lighting's nonexistent. Yet, there's the moon. Maybe he only got shots of Kai's back. . . . Should we call the police?"

Over my head, Mom said to him, "No police. Not now. It will just make things worse."

"I wasn't planning . . ." He stopped, and I could hear him take a deep breath. "Just talking things through. I see things clearer when I hear them. It . . ." He stopped, drew another big breath. "*I* take some getting used to."

Mom put her hand on his arm, which stopped his pacing. "We all take getting used to, Gerry. Now more than ever."

I asked everyone's forgiveness again, but couldn't forgive myself. Any time there was a lull in the conversation about what to do next, I mumbled, "I'm sorry, I'm sorry, I'm sorry," until finally after about an hour of it—or so it felt—Martha broke into one of my apologies with a voice like broken glass.

"No apologizing for lemons, girl. We gotta make lemonade. So says Dale Carnegie, and I agree."

That made Mom and Dr. Herks laugh, but I didn't understand what she meant. "Who's Dale Carnegie, and what does she mean?"

"He. That Dale's a he. And he means, we are stuck with the lemon, so deal with it." Martha was unstoppable. "It's a big lemon of a moment. Plenty of sour to go around. So what do we do with it? You can't eat it. So how are you going to use it?"

Finally, I got it. "Make lemonade."

"We've got to think about containment," Dr. Herks said.

I shook my head, because I didn't know what he meant.

"Circle the wagons," he added, which just made things murkier.

"Say it straight," Martha told him.

Mom sighed. "He means we've got to control the story."

"What story?" Martha gave a short, sharp laugh. "This isn't a story."

"It's a story *now*, Martha," I said. "It's going to be in the papers and maybe even on the news."

"Oh, *that!*" Martha shrugged. "Lemons."

"But how do we *make* the lemonade?" My voice sounded whiny. I felt as if I was five years old again.

"Squeeze out the juice, water it down, add sugar."

"But what does *that* mean?"

Mom answered for her, "We take the essence of the story and doctor it. We put our own spin on the story. We control the lemon *and* the lemonade."

"Not my job," Martha said, letting herself into the stall where Kai had sobbed himself to sleep. She closed the door to the rest of us and locked it behind her with a *snick*. It was as if she was saying we were the enemy as well.

And maybe we were.

☆ ☆ ☆

Dr. Herks wrestled a table out of the office and put it outside the stall. Mom and I brought out four chairs, though only three of us were sitting and talking.

We spoke in hushed tones about circuses, movies, Disney animal documentaries, and more, until Martha—in a fit of nosiness—came out of the stall. She didn't sit at the table with us, but instead paced up and down the corridor.

Dr. Herks kept slapping his hand on the table like some kind of punctuation. "There's always the local zoo," he said. "The one in Springfield."

I stood angrily. "That's just another way of saying Kai's a freak. I veto *all* these ideas!" My voice was harsh with lack of sleep. Dr. Herks hushed me with a finger to his lips.

"We're trying to think of ways to *protect* him, honey," Mom told me. She put out her hand and grabbed mine, but I shook her off.

"You're trying to find a way of displaying him, not containment but *entertainment*. He may be a freak—but he's *our* freak!"

"We're trying to keep him—and the farm—safe," Dr. Herks said. His pistol sat on the table, a reminder of how dangerous this all was becoming.

"Ari's right. Display is not protection," Martha said, coming out of the stall to sit in the chair put out for her.

I sat as well, too tired to remain standing.

"Keeping him in a stall forever is not good for his health," Dr. Herks reminded her. "He needs to run."

I nodded my agreement to them both, no longer trusting my voice.

The wind had picked up, and there was the sound of its swooshing through the tree limbs. We started to wrestle with the idea of getting onto radio and TV talk shows, the kids' shows, news shows. Mom and Dr. Herks sent ideas across the table as if they were playing a fast game of Ping-Pong.

All through the conversation, arms folded, Martha breathed noisily, like a winded horse, but made no suggestions. From the other side of the barn, a horse answered her back.

"Maybe what we need is a lawyer," Mom said. "I only have John Banks from town. He handles divorces. Not sure he's up to this."

"Maybe what we need is a *publicist*," said Dr. Herks. He said the "we" softly, as if he hadn't the right to use it and wanted Mom to know that he knew. Then he turned to me in case I didn't know what a publicist was. "Someone to help us sort through publicity and make sure it's good publicity, not bad."

Martha snorted again.

"Like it or not, Martha," Mom told her, "someone's going to try to exploit Kai. That's why *we* have to find ways to protect him."

And that's when I finally got it. Either he was taken care of by us, or he'd be taken over by people who only wanted to make money from him.

"We're going to need the backing of top veterinarians, folklorists, psychologists, professors . . . ," Dr. Herks said.

"Quacks, nuts, and academics." Martha stood up, shoving her chair roughly to one side.

"Don't you walk away from this, Martha," Mom said as Martha started down the corridor.

"Not walking here," Martha called back. "Running!"

Their voices were getting loud.

"Shhhh," I said, pointing at the stall. "You'll wake him." I spoke slowly, as if talking to children. "He needs time to grow up. He needs Robbie and me to play with him. He needs to learn."

"Learn what?" Mom asked.

"Learn what he likes—learn what he wants to be. And what he doesn't want to be. What if he became one of the bad centaurs in the Greek stories when he could be more like Chiron, who was a great teacher?"

"Ari's right, you know," Dr. Herks said. "We've been

thinking too much about keeping Kai hidden when we should have been thinking about what he could do to help himself once he's discovered."

Mom looked at him. "Oh my Lord!"

"What is it? Are you all right, Hannah?" He looked entirely stressed out. I wondered if he was going to faint again.

"I just realized that's what I've been doing with Robbie." She looked past Dr. Herks to me. "Keeping him hidden when I should have been thinking about—"

"Hannah, I never meant any such thing," Dr. Herks told her.

But I knew what to say. "Mom, Robbie *needed* that time with us here at the farm to do his learning, and now he knows how to talk to grown-ups as well as kids. He knows who he is. Maybe he should go to school next year. Doesn't Kai deserve the same?"

"She's right," Dr. Herks said. "Maybe we need to think about finding someone to teach and train him. Both of them, actually."

"Horse pucky!" Martha was back, shaking her finger at us. "There's no one who's got a horse like Kai, so how are they gonna train him better than I can? Or Hannah can?

In fact, they probably can't train him any better than Ari can."

"Thanks a lot," I muttered. But then I looked up. "That's it. We shouldn't train him as we do a horse. Because he's not a horse. And he's not a boy. He's both." I smiled for the first time since those flashes in the night. "Robbie saw that first. We have to teach Kai what we can. And he'll teach us the rest."

"I already knew that," said Martha, and once again she walked away.

Reporters

THE NEXT DAY WAS A GOOD DAY, or at least as good as a day can be when you believe something bad is about to happen and nothing does. We kept expecting phone calls that didn't come, riders who never showed to take their horses out for exercise, knocks on the door by police wanting to talk to the doctor with the gun, or groups of folks arriving to demand a viewing of the centaur.

But when nothing happened by the end of the day, we all started to relax.

Martha and I had let Kai run in the enclosed corridor until he was tired out. After a nap, we had him run again.

"Best thing for a young one," Martha said. "Get the jim-jams out."

"How would you know?" I asked.

"Oldest of six," she said.

It was the first time I'd ever heard her mention a family. I waited to hear more. But she was done with her surprises.

☆ ☆ ☆

Once dinner was over, Robbie and Kai read books together and then, with my evening chores finished, Robbie and I taught Kai how to play Monopoly. Since Kai had no idea what money was, or houses, hotels, jails, or trains, there was a lot of teaching and very little playing. It frustrated Robbie, who loved games, and I got really tired of explaining stuff that I thought everybody already knew, but Kai just took it all in eagerly.

Martha watched us from the doorway and was notably closemouthed. That should have been a warning to us all.

I began to yawn, and the yawns became contagious, so Martha shooed Robbie and me off to the house, and Dr. Herks said he'd stay the night in front of Kai's stall.

☆ ☆ ☆

Once in bed, I fell asleep and dreamed of Robbie all grown up, sitting tall on a horse, cowboy hat on his head.

There was music playing in the background, and he was staring past a high fence to a green meadow beyond. A sign on the fence read CENTAUR FIELD. It was night, and the sky was filled with shooting stars. Background music swelled. Everything felt right.

I was deep in the meadow-and-stars dream when a loud hammering made me bolt upright in bed. I woke to learn that the hammering was real and at our front door. Despite our positive attitude and yesterday's ease, everything had all gone wrong.

As Martha says, "Life bites your bottom when you're least expecting it."

It turned out there was a gaggle of reporters at the front door, from the *Boston Herald*, the *Boston Globe*, the UPI wire service, the *Greenfield Recorder*, and the *Daily Hampshire Gazette*.

Gaggle was Martha's word for it. "Like silly geese," she said later. "All honking and with no ideas of their own."

By the time I'd gotten dressed and downstairs, Mom had invited the reporters in for coffee. At least that stopped the noise.

"Oh, good, Ari, you're up," Mom said when I came into the kitchen looking for breakfast. "Go find Martha and Gerry, and then get your brother up and dressed."

I wanted to stay and hear what they were discussing, but she gave me the Look, which she reserved for special occasions. It meant *I really need you to do this now!*

So I ran out to Martha's house and banged on *her* door till she answered it, her hair startled into place with not one or two but *three* red rubber bands.

"Reporters," I said. "In the kitchen. Having coffee. I've got to get Dr. Herks."

Martha tucked her gray T-shirt into her jeans, slipped on her sneakers, exchanged the red rubber bands for one green, one blue, and ran past me, saying over her shoulder, "He's in the barn." Then she was gone, charging up the ramp and through our back door.

In the barn, I found Dr. Herks sitting in a chair in front of the stall, staring straight ahead and looking as if he had one of Martha's red rubber bands stretched around his head, tight enough to cause a massive headache. The table and other chairs had been moved back to where they belonged.

Grabbing him by the sleeve, I shook his arm. "Gerry, Gerry. . . ." When his eyes blinked, they weren't at all muzzy with sleep but wide and fierce. "Dr. Herks, it's Ari. We've got visitors."

"Who?" he barked. "Where?" as if he was still in the army.

"Reporters. Having coffee with Mom in the kitchen."

"Right!" he said. "You stay here."

"Mom told me to get Robbie up and dressed."

He nodded, stood. "Do what your mother says, only bring him out to the barn as soon as you can."

"I will."

Then he, too, was gone at a run.

I followed as quickly as I could, making my way past the kitchen door, where I could see a group of reporters eating Mom's blueberry muffins and guzzling coffee.

No one seemed to be talking. Yet.

✯ ✯ ✯

Robbie was already up and in a fresh T-shirt and pants. Mom always leaves his clothes at the foot of his bed. Usually he manages to dress on his own and get into the chair and wheel into the kitchen. But his chair was up against the far wall, which meant it must have rolled away in the night. Sometimes the brake wasn't set well enough, and the floors in this old house slope a bit. No matter how it had happened, it meant he hadn't been able to get into the chair on his own.

"What's all that noise?"

"Reporters. That's all I know." I pushed the wheelchair over so he could do his little bounce and roll into it, picking up a second book as he did so.

We went past the kitchen and out the back, and I wheeled him to the barn. He had a book of fairy tales with him. *The Olive Fairy Book.* "To read to Kai."

"Isn't that a bit over Kai's head?"

"Maybe today. Not tomorrow."

I ruffled his hair. "Smart guy!"

"He is."

"I meant you."

Robbie grinned up at me. "Kai's body is growing so fast, his brain must be growing fast, too."

"I get it. I get it! Now we're going out to the barn, and I'll bring you some breakfast in a few minutes. Better to eat it out here and not in the kitchen in front of the reporters. The company will be better in the stall."

"A lot better," he agreed.

☆ ☆ ☆

When we got to the barn, everything was quiet in the stall. Kai was still asleep, nestled up against Agora's rump, thumb in his mouth.

I left Robbie by the door in the stall with his books, *The Olive Fairy Book* and a biography of General Custer. He'd already opened it and was deep into the introduction. As I turned the corner at the end of the corridor, I heard a tiny *snick*. Robbie had locked the door behind me. I breathed out, suddenly aware I'd been holding my breath.

By the time I got back to the house, the coffee meeting was over, a bunch of cards were on the kitchen table with the reporters' names and phone numbers, and they were leaving in their various cars.

"What did you tell them?" I asked.

Mom smiled. "I said we had a desperately ill animal here, but by next Sunday, if it was well enough, they could come see for themselves whether the pictures their Mr. Fern was shopping around were real or not."

"So it *was* Fern," I said. "And he *did* get pictures."

Mom nodded. "Not great pictures," she said. "They were pretty gray and fuzzy, but enough to make the reporters very curious."

"They seemed okay with your mom's proposal,"

Dr. Herks said. "Especially since I told them I'd been up all night with the horse."

Martha snorted. "It was the straw in your hair that cinched it."

"Yes, the old hayseed trick," Mom said.

I gaped. "How did that get in your hair? You were asleep in the chair when I woke you."

He grinned. "Professional secret."

Clearly he'd been in to check up on Kai sometime during the night, maybe even slept in the straw, which had to be more comfortable than the chair.

"Robbie needs breakfast."

"Oh, right!" Mom began bustling around the kitchen and put together a hard-boiled egg, some toast with jam, and a large glass of milk. "You find something for yourself, Ari. I'll take this out to him."

"I'm off to the office," Dr. Herks said. "Don't want them to forget I'm the Big Dog. But I'll be back soon."

☆ ☆ ☆

I grabbed a bowl of cereal with bananas and wolfed it down, took a glass of milk with me, and finally went back to the stable. I hadn't realized how hungry I was until I started eating.

Mrs. Angotti was already out in the ménage with Joey. She was never this early, which was odd. Joey was up on Bor, who was still much too big for him to handle, so his mother, in her jodhpurs, was leading them around the ring.

Mom was standing by the fence watching, a letter in her hand. When she noticed me, she handed me the letter. "Mrs. A came super early to give me this. What do you think?"

Dear Mrs. Martins,

I meant no harm, really. And I told Zoe it was a secret. She didn't actally believe me anyway. So it wasn't really my fault her teacher sent it to the contest. But I'll take the blame. I'm really and truely sorry for any inconvenience I caused.

Angela

"So?"

"She misspelled two words," I said.

"I mean what do you think of what she says?"

"She's afraid of being told off, she's afraid of being banned from the farm, and she's never had to take the blame for anything in her life." I reread the letter quickly. "Also she doesn't know how to spell, which, for a junior in high school, is pretty bad." I took a deep breath. "Or else she just wrote the letter in a hurry because her mother made her, and she didn't take time to revise it. After all, she did spell *inconvenience* right!"

"Just because she's a lousy speller doesn't necessarily make her a bad person, honey. Maybe she really does feel sorry. Maybe she wouldn't hurt Kai for all the world."

I shrugged but didn't argue. It *could* be true. Stranger things had happened. I mean—we just had a centaur born in our barn.

Then I realized: Mom had confided in me and asked my opinion about something. I handed the letter back to her and smiled.

She folded the paper three times and put it in her pocket. "Angela said she'd take the blame."

"Then hold her to it."

Mom nodded. "I plan to. Nothing more needs to be said. And you have chores to do."

I saluted her, and we both laughed. Then I went to the barn to start mucking out the first of the stalls.

Kai's Run

FOR HALF A WEEK, things seemed to get back to normal, or at least to the *new* normal, which meant having less than half our usual riders and horses. Mom said we'd be all right, and maybe even more than all right once Kai had grown a little more and could hold his own with visitors.

He was already a huge hit with everyone in on the secret. So much so, we had to ration his visiting time. And the visitors had to be cautioned about feeding him too many apples and sugar cubes, especially the Angottis. He might have looked like a seven-year-old boy on the top, but he was still part foal and occasionally goofy.

Joey and Angela were allowed to visit Kai only with supervision, but the Proper kids were let in anytime they wanted to read to him.

Kai had to stay *in* the stall because we didn't dare let

him out for a run again, and the only thing he liked more than running turned out to be books. Robbie was reading him nonfiction about stars and constellations, about the history of the Morgan horse, and some novels as well. Kai couldn't seem to get enough of it.

"Can we bring a TV into the barn?" Robbie asked one night at bedtime. "Please, Mom—I think he'd especially like *Mister Ed*."

She smiled but shook her head. "We don't have the right kind of outlets to plug it in and no proper aerial out there. Also, we can't chance a TV man or an electrician in the barn asking questions, poking about. But I'll talk to Gerry. Maybe he'll have some ideas."

☆ ☆ ☆

Well, we all had ideas and not just about TV, but Dr. Herks had the best one. He came over that evening for dinner and told us.

"Kai is growing so fast. He needs to be able to run, not just stay cooped up in his stall or in the corridor. Agora's getting a little crabby, too. She tried to kick me this morning."

I gasped. That was not like Agora at all.

"Not a *real* kick," Dr. Herks was quick to say, "but a warning nevertheless."

"Why a fence?" Robbie asked. "Why not just let him run in the pasture?"

"Don't be a Silly Billy," Martha said. "Prying eyes. Secrets discovered. Crowds of people. Old man Suss selling tickets on his side of the fence."

"Martha's right. With a fenced-in run, Kai will be able to race to his heart's content outdoors," Dr. Herks told Robbie, "and yet be safe from prying eyes, as long as there aren't any photographers and sightseers in helicopters."

"*Helicopters?*" I checked his face to see if he was kidding.

☆ ☆ ☆

The next day, Friday, he showed up with a pickup truck full of wooden fencing, a posthole digger, a sledgehammer, and a toolbox.

"Taking a break from my practice" is how he put it. "For the first time in a year, I'm letting Dr. Small cover the office the entire weekend." He smiled. "That's how much I like your family, Ari."

I smiled back, afraid to read too much into what he'd said.

"I told her not to call me, not even if it's an emergency. And I reminded her she has always been great in emergencies. Since she's considering retirement, she's put more and more on my shoulders. I think she was shocked that I needed time off."

"Gerry, this"—Mom waved at the full pickup truck—"is hardly time off."

"It is to me," he said.

Mom smiled tentatively. "Thanks."

"Arlene's been a vet since before I was a teen," Dr. Herks explained. "I used to work for her cleaning out the pens. She's the one who encouraged me to go to veterinary school after my Vietnam service, and then let me buy into her practice. But she still needs to hear that she's a good vet as she worries that at her age she's lost too much of her speed and skill."

"Everyone does," Mom said. "I'm not as fast up on a horse these days . . ." She wasn't grinning, except with her eyes. I hoped Dr. Herks could see that.

★ ★ ★

We all helped with the fence—Mom and Martha and me, of course, as well as Mrs. Angotti, the Propers, and Dr.

Harries, who had come to work their horses and stayed to build the fence, not just the unloading of materials on Friday but the whole weekend long.

Dr. Harries and Mom and Mr. Proper hauled all the biggest pieces of fence to the places where Dr. Herks had dug forty postholes, twenty on each side, ten feet apart. I got to help Martha and Dr. Harries with the measurements.

"You women are too fast for me," Dr. Herks said, and gave me a wink.

The fence was eight feet high, higher than Kai would be when fully grown. It was attached to the end of the back barn but wound well into the pasture, staying far enough away from the Suss farm's fence that it couldn't be overlooked. It looped back on itself and—to make it a bit more interesting—cut off a corner of the pond so Kai would have a place to drink, too.

"Why not a jump or two?" Mrs. Angotti suggested when we were almost done.

"Too dangerous," Mom said.

Martha added, "You can't put a boy down if his leg breaks."

"Or get him into a wheelchair," Dr. Harries pointed out.

"Or have him use crutches," Mrs. Proper said.

The thought of all that was both funny and terrifying. The idea of any jumps was quickly dismissed.

Joey was more trouble than help until we let him sit in Agora's stall and play Monopoly with Robbie and Kai and the Proper kids. At this point, Kai could beat them all but had somehow figured out how to cheat in order to let Joey win occasionally.

The only one who stayed far away from the action was Angela. She elected to work in the kitchen making pitchers of lemonade and setting out the cookies for our frequent breaks. I think she was still embarrassed to be around us because of spilling the secret.

Either way, I was secretly relieved.

Even with all the help, getting that long fence up was hard work, and it took two days. We didn't finish until Sunday at dinnertime.

☆ ☆ ☆

That evening, we let Kai try out his new toy. He could go right from the barn into the fenced-in run without being seen by onlookers. The run was wide enough for him to turn around in, but not much more. It followed the curve of the wire fence, but only on the side where we bordered the National Forest land. We didn't want people over on the Suss property taking pictures from ladders.

He stepped into the run in a shy way. Unlike little boys, horses aren't really explorers. They prefer the known to the unknown. But soon enough, his boy brain took over and then Kai began trotting up and down, arms in the air and shouting, "I'm trotting fast, Ari." And when he broke into a gallop, he added, "I'm running *very* fast!"

As he raced along, tail flaring out behind, he called out, "The Black Stallion would be proud!"

You could always tell what he and Robbie were reading together!

"Not just fast, Kai—you're almost flying!" Then I called out the names of whatever gaits he was doing.

He already knew *walk, trot, gallop*, but we added *canter, pace, amble, halt, back up, turn* and he got them all the first time. The only one that confused him was the fox-trot because it went diagonally. We all laughed ourselves silly as he tried to master it.

Robbie made up a game song for him, trying to trick him.

Here comes Kai a-walking, walking,
Here comes Kai a-trot.
Here comes Kai ambling—
A canter, it is not!

"He's a pony Einstein," Mrs. Proper declared, patting his head each time he made the circuit.

Robbie got pouty at that. "Not a pony, not a scientist."

Mrs. Proper smiled. "You're right, Robbie. I won't make that mistake again."

But Kai wasn't hurt by what she said. In fact, he wanted to know what an Einstein was, and later we found him two children's books at the library on the subject.

Dr. Herks lent him two other books, one called *Essentials of Human Anatomy* and one about horse anatomy. They were both way over his head, but he loved the pictures.

"He just gulps it all down," Dr. Herks said. "Never saw anything like it."

"He'll be a teen before we know it," Martha said, adding sourly, "Not sure I'm ready for that!"

☆ ☆ ☆

It had become clear very early on that Kai had to be a vegetarian. He liked the taste of just about anything, but it turned out he had only one stomach after all. Dr. Herks had determined that by a variety of tests. One stomach, and it was in the horse part of his body.

There'd been a close call midweek, when Joey—feeling generous after having beaten Kai at Monopoly—had shared his chocolate cupcake with Kai, who wolfed it down. There was no way either of them could have known that chocolate can be very dangerous to a young horse's digestion.

Martha said, "Thank the stars that Dr. Herks was around and noticed a chocolate smear on Kai's mouth."

Thank the stars indeed! He got Kai to throw up the chocolate and explained what a close call we'd had. It convinced us all that Kai had to remain on a strict horse diet, and he had to learn what was safe for him to eat and why.

What Kai liked best (besides chocolate, which he now knew he couldn't have) were carrots and apples. He had a terrible sweet tooth, and would have eaten as many sugar cubes as he could get.

Dr. Herks told him sternly, "Not too often, Kai, because horses simply can't tolerate a lot of it."

"But Boy Kai likes sugar."

"It's horse Kai's tummy we have to worry about," Martha said.

That left grass and grains, which horses need because of ulcers and other stomach problems. So we had to give Kai oat cereals and breads made with rough oats, alfalfa, barley. From early on, Mom did one large baking on Wednesdays and smaller ones throughout the week. Now Angela helped whenever she was visiting.

It turned out that if we put enough molasses on barley mash, Kai would eat it like a dessert. For a treat he had oatcakes every Thursday with a dollop of apple butter. He called it *Yum-day*.

I got the job each evening to cook down a mixture of grasses, apple slices, unpeeled carrots sweetened with a little sugar water, and crushed vitamin pills Dr. Herks brought us to help strengthen Kai's bones. After the mixture cooled, I used a beater to turn it into a kind of puree and then poured it through a funnel into glass bottles, which we kept in a small refrigerator in his stall with a line snaking out to an outlet in the hall. It took him only a minute to learn how to open the refrigerator door. He could drink about a half dozen bottles of juice during the day. But all that food and the veggie-fruit drinks meant that his growth-spurt geyser became a constant waterfall. And as a consequence, he weaned himself.

Now that he was no longer nursing, Agora was put into another stall. Just as well since his boy stuff—a table for his games, a small bookcase, the fridge—was filling up all the spaces. Though often Kai asked for her to come back at night so he could sleep cuddled up next to her.

Luckily for me, he quickly learned to keep his stall clean. What with my other chores, I needed all the help I could get.

19

Questions, Answers

THE REST OF THE SIXTH WEEK FLEW BY, and Sunday almost all of the reporters, plus two new ones, came back. The only one who didn't was the guy from the *Boston Globe*, who sent us a message that he would use whatever the wire services gave him because he was on a bigger story: President Johnson had recently announced a huge new number of soldiers were being sent to Vietnam, and the *Globe* reporter was preparing to be sent overseas.

Mom invited the reporters into the barn office and gave them coffee and zucchini muffins. While they ate, she outlined what would happen next. It had taken us a couple of hours to figure it out, and she'd typed up the schedule. Dr. Herks had one of those new copying machines called a Xerox at his office, a present from a happy horse owner whose prize racehorse he'd saved. With it, he'd made a dozen copies, which he handed out. They were much easier to read than the purple mimeo things we had at school.

And then the questions came thick and fast.

"Is he real?" asked the first reporter, a redhead with an even redder mustache that covered the sides of his mouth like parentheses.

Mom's smile was tight. "Of course he's real. As real as you or me."

"I mean, a real *centaur*," the reporter persisted.

"*Pony boy* would be more accurate," Dr. Herks told him. "This isn't ancient Greece, after all."

A second reporter, slight and balding, with a nose like a leprechaun's, leaned forward and asked eagerly, "When can we see him?"

"Shortly," Mom said. "Kai should have finished his breakfast by now."

"Kai?" asked a guy with long stork legs and a nose like a beak.

Mom nodded at me to answer this one.

"That's his name. Short for Chiron, after the good centaur in the Greek myths, the one who taught Jason and other Greek princes."

A hand shot up. The man had a short, pointed beard. "Can you spell Chiron?"

I was surprised that a reporter had to ask such a thing, but I spelled *Chiron* slowly, the way you do in a spelling bee. They all scribbled in their notebooks.

Martha added, "And *her* name is Arianne Martins, daughter of the house and three-time winner of the Swift River Elementary School spelling bee."

Surprised, I blushed. I hadn't known she knew. Or cared.

More scribblings.

Mom then took over again. "We have ladders at five different locations along the fence so you can watch Kai run. Please don't call or shout to him. He's still very young and can startle easily. And no pictures outside, as he's already had a fright once. When he's back in the barn, in more comfortable and controlled surroundings, you will be able to speak to him, and that's where you can take your pictures."

There was a squabble of hands and voices.

The stork man asked, "He talks?"

And the bearded man added, "In English?"

Mom nodded.

"What else?" I muttered. "He was born here. Of course he speaks English!"

Mom glared at me.

"What does he think of the news about the soldiers going to Vietnam?" asked the redhead.

Martha huffed through her nose. "Don't be an idiot. He's a little boy. He loves fairy tales and board games. He's a whiz at Monopoly, and he recently stopped playing peekaboo. He doesn't watch the news. Or read the trash you write."

She stalked off, her shoulders hunched as if she thought they were about to throw paper bombs at her.

After she left, Dr. Herks gave them a quick rundown on Kai's anatomy, his diet, and the fact that he had two hearts.

That's when the balding guy said, "So what's this about . . ." He looked down at his notebook. "*Puericentaurcephalitis*? Is it catching? Is it fatal? Can humans—"

"Where did you hear that?" Dr. Herks almost barked at the man.

"Not at liberty to give you my sources."

"Well," Dr. Herks said slowly, almost as if he was also reluctant to give his sources. Then he grinned. "It means 'boy horse disease' in dog Latin, and I just used that made-up term to buy us time. None of us had ever seen anything like Kai before."

"You're kidding," the reporter said.

Almost jumping in his wheelchair to have a say, Robbie put in, "He was kidding then. He's not kidding now."

The reporters looked over at Robbie, and all of a sudden seemed interested in a different story.

Dr. Herks called them back to the major story. Then after insisting they leave their cameras on the desk—which they did somewhat reluctantly—Dr. Herks turned to the door. "We'll go outside now."

They followed him out, looking for all the world like ducklings in a row.

★ ★ ★

The reporters went up their assigned ladders carefully. Dr. Herks climbed the fifth one to keep a careful eye on everything. Mom, Robbie, and I were stationed by the gate connecting the barn to the run.

Martha led Kai out, one hand on his shoulder, speaking softly to him.

Before opening the gate, Mom looked at Kai carefully. She took the rubber bands out of his hair and gave his curls a quick brush. "There will be people up on the ladders to watch you run." She used only one of the rubber bands to pull the hair away from his face. "You need to see where you're going," she said.

"Going fast?"

"Yes, and people will see how fast you are going."

"Mrs. A?" Unaccountably, Kai liked her. I think he found her constant babble soothing. "Joey?"

"No," I told him, "new people. They want . . . they want to admire you."

"Okay," he said brightly. "What's *admire*?"

Robbie put in, "They want to watch you run and see how wonderfully you do it. They may even cheer or clap their hands."

I added, "Let's show them how we play the walk-trot-canter-amble game."

He smiled at that. "I *like* that game! I like Robbie's songs, too."

Robbie glowed.

So Mom opened the gate, and Kai trotted in.

The minute he rounded the bend where the first two ladders were positioned, the reporters gave startled gasps, and one said a word I'm not supposed to know. Or use.

But unfazed, Kai broke into a canter, arms spread wide,

crying out as he often did, "I'm going fast, Ari. See how fast I'm going!"

I called back, "The Black Stallion would be proud of you, Kai."

His voice reached me from the far end of the run, "And the Island Stallion, too." Then he turned and came galloping back for his hug and his first bottle of juice and oatcake of the day.

After he ran back and forth a few times, I called out the gaits—walk, trot, canter, gallop. I mixed the order up a bit. He never missed one. Not even the fox-trot, which he'd been practicing. It may have looked difficult to the reporters, but to Kai it was basic stuff.

High up on their ladders, forgetting Mom's warning about noise, the reporters clapped loudly and called Kai's name.

At the end, out of sheer excitement from all the applause, Kai tried something I'd never seen him do before. He rose on his hind legs and pawed at the air!

At that, everyone cheered—the reporters, Dr. Herks, Martha, Robbie, Mom, and me. So Kai did the hind leg stand a second time, but he was tired enough that he was a little wobbly. Martha dashed into the run and grabbed his hand, saying, "Enough for one day, I think."

I handed him another bottle of his juice, and he guzzled it down, saying in between sips, "I like the clapping, Ari."

"I can see you do."

"Just don't get to like it too much," Martha told him.

"Why?"

"It'll make your head swell."

"Will that hurt?"

"No," I said, smiling at him, "but it will make it hard to wear a hat."

"I don't have a hat," he said. "Can I get a hat?"

"You can have my Red Sox baseball cap," Robbie said.

"What are the Red Sox?"

"A team that doesn't win much," Martha said. "Now, into the barn for a rubdown. Look at you, all sweated up and tired."

"I'm not tired," he insisted.

But we could all see he was by the way his tail dragged.

Once back in the stall, Mom wiped down Kai's horse parts with a towel, but he used a second towel to wipe the sweat off his arms and chest himself. Then he changed T-shirts.

"Can I have an apple, Ari?" he asked.

"Sure," I said, taking one from the pocket of my jacket. "And now we need to talk to the reporters."

"The ones who cheered me?"

"The very ones," Mom said.

"Good!" Kai said, though he held a hand up to his face and yawned behind it.

Mom called to Dr. Herks, who brought the reporters in but warned them that as soon as they were done, "this little pony boy will be taking a nap."

The interview went well. Kai allowed the reporters to touch his hands and his haunch, and look at his legs. The stork man even asked if he could feel Kai's hair.

"Why?" asked Kai.

Stork shrugged. "I just . . . I just . . ."

"Sure."

He answered the questions he could—what he ate, where he slept, what he did all day.

"I eat like a horse," Kai said, grinning to show he got the joke. "I eat grains and grasses and apples and carrots." He nodded toward Dr. Herks. "And no chocolate. It makes me sick. Sometimes Dr. Herks lets me have sugar. But not often." He smiled slyly. "Not often *enough*!"

Dr. Herks explained Kai's diet then, and about how tender horse stomachs could be.

"So no pizza or ice cream?" said the reporter with the beard.

"Afraid not," Dr. Herks said.

Someone asked what languages Kai spoke beside English.

"Horse."

The redheaded reporter asked him to say something in Horse, so Kai gave them half a minute's worth of whinnying and snorting.

"What does that mean?"

"You wouldn't understand."

"Try me."

Kai turned and looked at me. "Why should I *try* him?"

"Next question," said Dr. Herks.

"Tell us about your mother," the bald one said.

"I have *three* mothers." Kai pointed to Martha and Mom. "And Agora." He waved his hand at the side of his stall.

"Our pony," Mom explained. "She gave birth to him."

"I call her Mama," Kai said. "In Horse, she's called . . ."

And here he did a long, sweet whinny that ended with a series of three snorts.

"What does that mean?" the redheaded reporter asked.

"It means the Short One with the Long Temper, and Look Out for Her Heels!" This time Kai grinned mischievously.

"When someone she doesn't like gets too close, she kicks," Martha explained. "Fair warning."

"I have a father." Kai nodded at Dr. Herks. "A sister," smiling at me. "And a brother." He gestured toward Robbie in the corner. Robbie waved.

The reporters took it as an invitation to ask about Robbie.

Stork man turned to me. "Why is he in a wheelchair?"

"Why not ask him yourself? He's not dumb." I said it more sharply than I meant. Well, maybe not more than I *meant*, but probably more than I should.

Dr. Herks rolled Robbie's wheelchair next to Kai.

Robbie leaned forward. "My mother was given thalidomide when she was pregnant with me."

I think he wanted to match Kai's openness with the reporters. But I could almost hear them thinking *seal child*, and felt my shoulders hunch defensively. "My brother happens to be in a wheelchair," I said, rather too loudly. "But that's not *who* he is. He's smart, funny, perceptive, and sweet."

"Wow, thanks, Ari," Robbie said.

Then remembering the new word I learned when researching centaurs, I added, "He's liminal."

"Is that part of his condition?" the bearded reporter asked.

"Don't be stupid," the stork man said. "It has something to do with werewolves."

I nodded. "That's right. It means someone caught between"—I made my fingers into quote marks—"*two contrasting natures.* Like . . . like a werewolf. Or like a faun. Or a centaur." I gave a half smile. "Or a selchie."

"Hey—spelling champ, spell that last thing," said the redhead, so I did.

"What's a selchie, then?" the bearded guy asked.

"A selchie is a mythical creature who's a human on land and a seal in the sea."

"Neither one of these kids looks mythical to me," said the stork guy.

I liked him, stork legs and all. "Just . . . different," I said.

"Maybe better," Kai added. "I can run fast. And my brother makes up songs."

"Can we hear one of the songs?" The bearded man tried to make his voice sweet, but it didn't work particularly well.

Kai and Robbie whispered, and then together they sang the walking-trotting-galloping song. Kai's flutelike voice took off on a descant and Robbie's steady, deeper tones anchored the tune. They must have sung it together before, but it was the first time I'd ever heard them do it.

I looked at Mom, and she had an *ahhhhh* expression on her face. Dr. Herks did, too.

With that, the interview was over. The reporters got to take pictures of all of us, and off they went.

And Kai, as predicted, shortly fell asleep.

Back at the house, Robbie did the same.

It had been a long day.

20

An Unexpected Visitor

IN THE MORNING, the stories were in more papers than we could count since the UPI wire was picked up by newspapers and magazines all across the world. Dr. Herks bought as many as he could find in Northampton and Amherst and brought them over.

Each story was part true and part made up. One said Kai was a teen, another that he was a toddler. One said he was well-muscled, another that he was a hunchback. One article reported that he snorted like a horse and sweated like one, too. A woman reporter who hadn't even been there wrote a story about how his hair was as stiff as a mane, and another story said it was as soft as a child's. The only thing they seemed to agree on was that he had a horse's body with four legs and a tail, but a human torso, two human arms, and a human face.

No one mentioned Robbie.

Each story had an extra bit of information that we hadn't told them. Mom said they must have had it in some old files.

Martha looked unamused. "Talking to neighbors," she said.

Some led with that bit of information; some ended with it: "Mrs. Martins is the ex-wife of rock-and-roll superstar and bad boy, the single-named Wolf, currently on an East Coast tour."

We were famous.

We were infamous.

We were overwhelmed.

☆ ☆ ☆

The day after the papers hit the newsstands, we began to understand what our new life was going to be like.

I was dressed and wheeling Robbie in for breakfast before starting my chores. He'd been chattering about the new book he and Kai were reading together, a biography of George Washington, when I heard Mom arguing heatedly in the kitchen with someone. I assumed it was another reporter or Mrs. Angotti.

Instead, it was someone I hadn't seen in quite a while.

Six years, actually. But I knew him at once.

"Dad!" I said as we came into the kitchen.

He hadn't changed at all, except that now he had a tattoo of a snarling wolf on his right arm, and his hair was much more gold than I remembered. I wasn't sure if I was happy or angry he was here.

Another man stood near the table, not the sort of person my father ever hung out with when he lived with us. Most of them had been scruffy musicians with long hair, and their mascara-eyed girlfriends. This man was well dressed, in a dark suit and tie, plus a pocket handkerchief that matched the tie. His hair was thinning a bit, and when he smiled, his teeth were very even and bright.

"Hi, Princess. You're so grown up and beautiful. I've missed you tremendously. I think about you every day," Dad said.

Every day? He thought about me every day? Then why hadn't he come back to tell me before this? Why hadn't he sent any letters? Invited me to one of his concerts? Why hadn't he phoned?

He shot me a charming smile, and I realized it was his stage smile. I guess I was now old enough to understand that his eyes were not charming and sparkling with any love, but calculating the effect he was having on me.

And calculating something else as well, which I found out in the very next sentence.

"Haven't we hit the jackpot here!" There was a sweetness in his voice that seemed made up, as if he was acting a part. He refused to look at Robbie.

"*We've* hit nothing," Mom said. "Unless it's rock bottom, having you back here. Just another one of your schemes, Les. The ones that used to drag me in. And nearly killed me until you left—"

"*Dragged* you in? You begged me to take you with me wherever I was going, Han." His face had gotten flushed. Spots of color like clown makeup blossomed on his cheeks. "You wanted out of that small-minded ivory tower college town where your professor daddy taught. You saw me as the knight in shining armor come to rescue you from boredom."

"*Jackpot?*" It was the one word he'd spoken that seemed . . . well, genuine. The one true word he'd really meant in his compliments to me. Because the meanness that had just sprayed out of his mouth made everything that had come before a lie.

He spread his arms wide, as if I was the audience at one

of his shows. "We've got a gold mine here if that horse thing is real and not some Disney animatroon . . . animatronic," he said. "You know, Princess, I saw one of those things at the World's Fair when I played there last year." He gazed at me as if no one else mattered. "Yeah, I get to do cool stuff like that, Princess. And that animatronical thing looked just like Abe Lincoln. Moved in a herky-jerky way, but kinda cool, too. You'd love it."

He must have thought I was still seven. Maybe in his eyes I was. But he didn't see the real me, the one who grew up when he wasn't there.

He went on without a clue. "So you see, I need to know if this pony-boy thing is the real deal. If it is, we could have a major movie here or a TV series, like *Lassie* or *Rin Tin Tin*, plus stuffed animals, lunch boxes." He did the smiley thing at me again. The smile that never really got to his eyes. "You'd like a lunch box like that, wouldn't you, Princess?"

"I'm in junior high, Dad. We don't have lunch boxes. We have a cafeteria."

As if he hadn't heard my answer, or didn't care, he said, "Well, maybe a breeding program then."

"*Breeding* program? Kai's not two months old!"

He bent toward me, as if we were close. "*Is it?*" he asked.

I backed away. "Is it *what*?"

"Is it real?"

"*It's* a he," Robbie said. "His name is Kai. And he's as real as you are."

The wolf who was our father ignored Robbie. He was now close enough that I could smell something bitter on his breath. I wondered if he'd been drinking. Biting my lower lip, I moved away, as if whatever he had was catching. "A *lot* realer than you, Dad."

"Ouch," he said, and smiled again, but not as broadly. "You sure know how to hurt a guy. Like your mother that way. She broke my heart."

"You were the one that left, Les," she reminded him.

"Wolf," the suit man said, "let me do the talking. I'm your lawyer. It's my job." He turned to Mom and held out his hand. "My name is Daniel Pickens, of Pickens, Berlin, Hyatt, and Temple."

Mom shook his hand.

Still smiling, my father took a seat at the kitchen table, looking more and more wolflike every minute. His smile was starting to turn into a snarl as he worked at it, showing too many teeth.

"Tell them," he said to Mom, "tell them how this is *my*

house and *my* land and therefore *my* little monstrosity in the barn there."

"You gave me this place," Mom said quietly. "Sent me a letter and said you never wanted to see it or me again. Said I was only good at making girl babies and . . ." She thought a minute about what to say next, then said it very quietly as if it soiled her mouth. "And monstrosities. You seem to like that word." She took a deep breath before continuing. "As for breaking your heart, that would have been impossible. You never had one. You're as animatronic as that Abe Lincoln you sang with."

"Nice to see *you* haven't changed, Mrs. Smart-Mouth College Girl," Dad snapped at her.

"Wolf," Mr. Pickens said, "let me remind you again. *I* do the talking."

Ignoring his lawyer's advice, my father said, "I never sent any such letter."

Mom sighed. "You have an awfully convenient memory, Les. But *I* have a filing system, something my college professor daddy taught me. You did indeed send that *lovely* note along with the divorce papers—which I read, gave to my lawyer, signed, copied for the file, and sent back."

She glanced over at Robbie and me to make sure we were all right with what we were hearing.

I'd already grabbed Robbie's little three-fingered hand and now gave it a gentle squeeze. How could we know if we were all right? Maybe Mom didn't talk about the wolf, didn't actually say a bad word about him either to me or to Robbie, though I'd overheard her tell Martha once or twice, when the subject had come up, that "rubbing a wound only makes it worse."

He leaned forward again and gave her a look that scared me. "I never signed any papers. You never put a penny into this place. It all comes from *my* earnings. You get a check from me every month, lady. Blood money. I'm amazed the farm's still running. You may have been well educated, Han, studying literature and all, but you never did have a lick of sense then or now about how the real world works."

"Wolf!" Mr. Pickens said, anger in his voice. "Zip it!"

The meanness of what my father was saying just about took my breath away. I knew how hard Mom worked to keep the farm going. To keep Robbie and me safe. To teach Robbie all he would need to know about dealing with the world.

Tears welled up in my eyes, but as soon as they started, they stopped. Seems I was too mad to cry.

Mom glanced over at me again and recognized something on my face. "You've just lost your daughter for good," she told him, "and she and your son were the only wonderful things you ever helped bring into this world."

"I make music," he said. "I make people happy with my songs."

"I only have your word that you make people happy. But I do know for certain that you never made *us* happy— Ari and Robbie and me." She stood up, went over to the desk, opened a secret drawer that even I hadn't known existed, and pulled out an envelope. She handed it to Mr. Pickens.

He put on a pair of half-glasses that made the bottom of his eyes bigger than the tops, and skimmed the contents of the envelope. Then he read the papers again, slowly this time. At last, turning, he glared at my father.

"Wolf," he said, "you told me there was nothing in writing."

"I didn't sign any papers," my father said. "Just like I told you."

Mr. Pickens shook the letter at him. "But you signed this letter. And here's a copy, duly notarized, of the divorce papers."

"I didn't write any letter."

I'm sure my mouth was gaping open. The lawyer was holding the very letter, and my father kept saying it didn't exist.

"It's got your signature," Mr. Pickens said, shaking the letter again at him. "A signature I know all too well."

"Then I must have been drunk at the time. Or high."

"Legally, being under the influence of either alcohol or drugs is no excuse. Especially as the letter shows no proof of that. And trust me, you don't want to say that sort of thing in front of a judge, or—may I remind you—in front of anyone except me! Furthermore, technically, you *did* desert your wife and children."

I'd never heard anyone use *furthermore* in an actual sentence before.

"One child," my father said. "A girl. I couldn't possibly have fathered that other one." He didn't look at Robbie when he said it.

Mom looked up at the ceiling. "Children. Both your children."

He scowled. "The baby was as good as dead before I left, so technically I only deserted my wife and daughter. How was I to know he would manage to live?"

How indeed? I thought, remembering when I first knew that he wasn't coming back, thinking it had to have been my fault, that I hadn't been good enough or sweet enough or—

"You'd seen Robbie only once in the hospital, and he was joyously alive," Mom said. "He's still the most joyous child I've ever known."

I gave Robbie's hand another squeeze. He squeezed mine back.

The wolf stood and loomed over her. He's five foot nine, and Mom is . . . well . . . she's not anywhere near that big. "You should have had that *thing* aborted when we found out about the pills. . . ."

I went cold. I could feel sweat on Robbie's palm.

Mr. Pickens came over to stand between them. "I'm not liking what I'm hearing, Wolf. There are two children involved. *Your* children. You and I are leaving right now before you make it any worse. And this letter—"

"That letter was private between me and my wife."

Mr. Pickens smiled, one of those mouth-twisting, this-is-not-funny smiles. "There's nothing private here apart from your conversations with me."

"Besides, *I've* been listening and heard it all," said a new voice, very grimly. Dr. Herks was standing in the door, body taut, as if ready to explode. I wondered how long he'd been standing there.

"The letter," Mr. Pickens emphasized, "says exactly what your wife just said."

"Ex-wife!" Mom was emphatic.

Mr. Pickens sighed. "*Girl babies and monstrosities*. Wolf, if that phrase gets out to the press, you can kiss your career good-bye."

"My lawyer's on her way, Hannah," Dr. Herks said quietly, "if you want to talk to her." He must have used the barn phone.

"Thanks, Gerry, but I think we're done talking."

"Who's *he*?" my father demanded, looking directly at Dr. Herks.

"Dr. Herks, the vet," I said. "The one who's been taking care of Kai." In my head I added, *Taking care of us, too.*

"Ari, take Robbie outside," Mom said. "There's something more I want to say to your father, and I don't want you two hearing it."

"But, Mom—"

"Come on, Ari," Robbie said. "Something smells awful in the kitchen. It'll be sweeter in the barn." Which was the snarkiest thing I'd ever heard him say.

Just before we left, I turned to look back. Mr. Pickens was handing his card to Dr. Herks. Mom stood with her arms folded across her chest, stone-faced. My father was doing his wolf imitation, snarling. It was the sort of scene our English teacher calls a tableau.

As I pushed Robbie along, he made up a little song which probably comforted him, but it didn't help me at all.

> *My brother is a horse,*
> *And I am a seal.*
> *No big deal, nope, no big deal.*
> *It's not the way you look that counts,*
> *It's the way you feel, the way you feel.*
> *It's what makes you real, boy,*
> *Makes you really real.*

He sang it all the way to the barn.

Monsters

WHAT I DIDN'T KNOW UNTIL LATER was that my father and mother argued for a few minutes more, about money and about the farm and about visitation rights. For me, not for Robbie.

He called Mom some awful names and accused her of things like having boyfriends and not declaring how much the farm made on her taxes and other things he simply made up. He even—or so I learned much, much later—accused her of trying to sabotage his career and hiring someone to kill him. Mr. Pickens finally had to drag him away, but not before my father slammed the door so hard, it almost came off its hinges.

Dr. Herks heard him say to Mr. Pickens, "You go wait in the car. I've got something to take care of first," but by then Dr. Herks was so busy soothing Mom that he didn't get outside right away. Besides, he figured that the lawyer could handle it, since he'd already shown us how he could shut my father up.

Maybe love makes you blind to danger. Or maybe love makes all our choices hard ones.

✮ ✮ ✮

Robbie and I were already back in Kai's stall. Except for the little song, Robbie and I hadn't spoken a word since leaving the house.

The familiar smell of horse brought us back to ourselves, our real lives. Not the lies that our father had made up about us. I unlocked the door, and we slipped in.

Agora was casually munching on oats, because nobody had gotten around to moving her back into her own stall that morning. Ignoring her, Kai was standing in a corner reading the George Washington book.

He looked up and grinned at us. "George Washington did *not* cut down a cherry tree," he said. "That was just a made-up story."

I laughed, but it quickly turned into something else when I heard noises coming from the other side of the barn—horses whinnying in alarm, someone cursing loudly.

I knew at once who it had to be.

"Robbie," I said, "stay here with Kai and Agora. Keep the door locked. I'll see what's going on, and if I have to, I'll get Dr. Herks."

Without checking through the blinds first, I opened the door and was about to slip through it when someone pushed past me as if he hadn't even noticed I was there.

"Where's my little jackpot?" he said. "Where's the answer to my money woes? You'd better be real." His words were slurring, and he seemed crazed. Or drunk. Or both.

He shoved Robbie aside so hard the wheelchair tipped, and Robbie tumbled to the floor. Luckily, there was a lot of straw to cushion his fall, but the chair fell on top of him, pinning him against the wall.

"Ari! Ari!" he called out, in a panicky voice.

I ran toward him, but before I could help, the wheelchair was lifted up by Kai as if it was no more than a toy. Setting the chair to one side, he kneeled on his forelegs and picked Robbie up, cradling him in his arms, saying, "Don't be sad, Brother. Kai is here."

Robbie was sniffling, but rubbed his eyes with the back of his three-fingered hand.

My father took in the scene and suddenly understood that it was Kai, the pony boy, kneeling before him. "My little monster!" he crowed and threw his arms wide as if to embrace both Robbie and Kai.

I started to bend over, to check that Robbie wasn't badly hurt. As far as I could tell, no bones broken, no blood. Just a little scared, and now a lot mad.

That's when the wolf man said, "So you're coming with me, monster," as he reached down for Kai's mane.

I put out a hand to stop him. "The only monster here is *you*, Dad."

He made a fist. I thought he was going to punch me, and I didn't know what to do. I closed my eyes and flinched.

But Agora had had enough. She trotted over, turned her back to him, and kicked up and out with all her might.

Look Out for Her Heels, indeed!

If Agora had been a horse, she might have caught him in the chest and broken some serious bones. But she was only a pony, and her hooves hit him farther down.

He sure screamed a lot for a grown man.

Hobbling out of the stall, he yelled for his lawyer. "Daniel! Daniel Pickens! Get over here now!" His voice began rising higher, almost if he was singing. "I'll sue you for assault, Hannah. I'll have this farm and everything you own. Daniel, get over here. I need to go to the hospital right away!"

I ran out after him, tears flooding my eyes. Not tears for me. Not even tears for Robbie or Kai. But for my father, who would never be able to make his way back to us after this. Not that we wanted him to—not ever.

He never looked back, just climbed into his car, a bright red Corvette convertible, and, with his lawyer in the passenger seat, spun out of the driveway. It rained gravel.

When I returned to the stall, Agora was once again head down in her oats bucket, placidly munching away. In the corner, Kai—a bit awkwardly—was helping Robbie up onto his back while Robbie clutched his mane. They both saw me at the same time.

"Look, Ari!" Robbie called. "I can ride, too!"

"Robbie, that's—" I began, meaning to say how dangerous it was.

"Not without a helmet, young man!" It was Mom behind me. Behind *her* stood Dr. Herks. And behind *him* was Martha.

"And not until you learn how to do it right," Martha said. I wasn't sure if she was talking to Robbie or to Kai.

Dr. Herks plucked Robbie from Kai's back. "Kai's still

too young to carry this much weight. It will hurt his back and harm his legs. But at the rate he's growing, I bet you'll be able to ride him safely by the fall."

As he brought Robbie back to his wheelchair, Dr. Herks added to Mom and Martha and me, "It's not just the boy part that's growing fast, his horse half is growing at a phenomenal rate, too. He's already taller than Agora, just not filled out."

"That's because he's *magic!*" Robbie said. "And when I'm on his back, I'm magic, too."

Magic. What I'd always wanted.

Besides, it turned out to be the best explanation we were ever to get.

✯ ✯ ✯

Back in the kitchen, we talked about what had just happened, and who had hurt whom.

"He didn't really hurt me, Mom," Robbie said. "Except my feelings."

"Well, Agora hurt *him!*" I'm embarrassed to say I grinned at the memory.

"Then I hope he has to go into the hospital." Martha was busy pulling the rubber bands out of her hair and combing out the snarls with her fingers. "Hospitals can make you sick, you know. Doctors, too."

Dr. Herks laughed.

"Oh, not you, Herkel," she said. "You're not that kind of doctor."

Mom shook her head. "Hospitals make you *well*, Martha."

"A lot *you* know. When have you ever been in a hospital?"

Mom got that exasperated look on her face, her forehead crossed with lines like notebook paper. She held up her hands and started counting on her fingers: "Appendix, tonsils, Arianne, Robbie, oh—and a bout of pneumonia when I was a child, and a broken arm from falling off a horse when I was fifteen. Is six times enough?"

Martha gave a loud humph, and Dr. Herks laughed again.

He's enjoying this way too much, I thought. But with very little urging, he called his lawyer, and we all listened in shamelessly, at least to his part of the conversation.

Afterward, he assured us that Mom's insurance would probably cover any doctor bills that a horse of hers inflicted. Furthermore, Dr. Herks' lawyer doubted Dad's lawyer would ever let him sue us, given the fact that Dad had as good as assaulted his daughter and his handicapped son, and had been vocal about his plans to steal a valuable asset from his ex-wife's farm (Kai). Plus the knowledge that Dad's reputation could be ruined by any revelation of what had happened here would—Dr. Herks' lawyer said—"guarantee his silence."

Still, she promised to give Mr. Pickens a call in about an hour just to be sure.

And so we weathered two storms—the reporters and *Wolf Hurricane*, as Robbie called it.

22

Plan A+

THAT NIGHT, exhausted by the day's revelations, I fell into a deep sleep and had the same dream again: Robbie sitting astride a horse, looking tall and whole.

I woke up, and it was still dark. The clock said it was twelve thirty, but I didn't feel sleepy at all. In fact, I was incredibly excited about my dream and what I thought it meant. So I got up, put on my robe and slippers, and went into Mom's room to tell her all about my idea before I forgot it or dismissed it as just a dream.

She wasn't there.

Robbie? I thought. *Kai?*

And then the worst thought of all: *Dad's come back!*

I kicked off the slippers and was heading toward Robbie's room when I heard a noise in the kitchen. It was Mom, and it sounded as if she was crying.

I took off at a run. "Mom!" I shouted.

She was sitting at the kitchen table, a cup of tea in front of her. Dr. Herks was on his knees on the floor, a look of pain on his face.

"What's wrong?" My heart seemed to be pounding out a strange rhythm in my chest.

Dr. Herks looked up at me, then got laboriously to his feet. "I'll let you know when your mother gives me her answer."

"Answer?"

Mom's hands left her face. Tears ran down her cheeks. "Yes," she said. "That's my answer. Yes." She took a deep breath. "But only if the children agree."

Dr. Herks put his arms around her. "Let's start with Ari."

"What's going on?" I asked, but my face was hot because I'd already guessed.

"I've asked your mother to adopt me," Dr. Herks said and winked.

I laughed. "I don't need another brother, Dr. Herks," I said. "I need a dad."

He gathered me into their embrace. "Then you've got him. But only if you call me Gerry."

That's when I remembered why I'd been looking for

Mom and pulled away, trying to look serious, which was hard because I had this ridiculous grin threatening to split my face in two. "Listen, I have an idea."

"Better than *this* one?" Gerry asked.

Holding hands, they looked at me with goofy smiles, maybe even goofier than mine. But I couldn't wait to tell them.

"Maybe," I said, "since it includes all of us."

"Go on," Mom said, and Dr. Herks . . . Gerry . . . said it at the same time.

"So, I had a really strange dream several nights ago and now again." I told them all about it. They looked at me oddly, as if I'd gone crazy or something.

"Ari . . . ," Mom began. "It's nearly one in the morning."

"No, Mom, listen. I think it's about Robbie on Kai's back. Up there he had a kind of power. A kind of . . ." I waved my hands around as if I might pluck the word I was looking for out of the air.

Gerry nodded. "A kind of wellness?"

"Presence," Mom offered.

Taking a deep breath, I nodded and then spelled it out. "Maybe Kai could learn how to carry handicapped riders like Robbie, to help them become stronger in their bodies—and in their hearts."

Mom clapped her hands. "Yes!" she breathed. "Yes!"

Leaning toward me, Gerry grinned. "Arianne, it's brilliant. Why didn't *I* think of that?" He turned to Mom. "I've read about this sort of thing in Scandinavia. A woman—I can't remember her name—had had polio and couldn't walk without canes. But she'd been quite the horsewoman before and went back to riding as soon as she could. She even won a medal at the Helsinki Olympic Games for Dressage."

"You're talking about Lis Hartel," Mom said. "She won two silver medals."

"*That's* the name!"

Mom sucked in her upper lip, something she did when she was thinking hard. "There are a couple of places in America that do a kind of riding for the handicapped, though not around here. I never paid much attention. I thought Robbie would never be able to sit on a horse, much less ride. Even yesterday in the stall, seeing him on Kai's back, I didn't make that connection. I was too afraid he was going to fall."

"That's the beauty of it, Mom. With Kai's help—"

"We'll have to *ask* Kai," Gerry said. "Not *tell* him."

"Of course," Mom said. "Consensus."

"I can't imagine anything that would please him more.

Except . . ." I smiled. "Except maybe when he finds out you two are engaged! He already calls you his mom and dad."

They looked at each other as if ready to burst out laughing.

"So he does," Mom said.

Gerry added, "It's what gave me the courage to ask your mom to marry me."

They looked at each other again with those goofy smiles.

I turned to go upstairs and said over my shoulder, "I'm going back to sleep, you guys. My work here is done."

☆ ☆ ☆

I woke with such a sense of relief and joy, I couldn't wait to break the news about the marriage to the boys. I thought they'd probably be stunned.

Mom and I told Robbie and Martha about the proposal at breakfast.

Robbie didn't look stunned at all. "I wondered how long it would take him to ask. I knew you'd say yes, Mom."

"How come *I* didn't know?" I said.

"You were too busy hoping," he told me. "Instead of

paying attention to what was really happening." He turned to Mom. "Guess it's okay for me to call him Gerry now?" He smirked. "Or Dad! I've never had anyone to call Dad before. I think I am going to like that. A lot."

Then he burst into song.

Oh Dad, oh Dad,
The first and best
I've ever had.
A vet to care
For seal and pony
He will be our
One and only. . . .

"I made up that song a while ago when I figured it out."

"Pretty smart for a kid," I said.

As for Martha, she gave one of her huffing noises, folded her arms across her chest, and said, "It's high time we had some good news."

☆ ☆ ☆

We all trooped out to the barn to tell Kai, and he was just as unstunned as Robbie had been.

"Now Hannah Mom will be married to my dad," Kai said. "I like that."

"There's a question we need to ask you, Kai," I said. "It's about . . ." I stopped, not sure how to put it.

But Mom knew just what to say. "Kai—you know that everyone at a farm has a special job. We have an idea for yours. Or rather, it was Ari's idea."

"Tell me, tell me!"

"We think you could help children like Robbie, letting them ride, helping them have strength and faith in themselves," Mom said.

"You'd be their special friend—" I began, thinking he needed more encouragement.

"Today?" Kai squealed. "Can I start today?" He clapped his hands.

"When you're bigger and stronger," Mom said, "and we have all learned the best way to work together."

"I'm going to help," Robbie added.

"Help, shmelp," I said, "you two are going to *lead* the way."

Robbie was aglow with this thought.

"You know, it was you on Kai's back yesterday that gave me the idea. Oh, and the dream."

"What dream?" Robbie and Kai asked together.

So I told them.

"This new venture needs a name," Mom said. "How about the Robbie Foundation?"

Robbie shook his head. "No, it's not about me. It's about Kai." He looked up at the ceiling for a moment, then said, "How about Kai's Kids?"

★ ★ ★

We waited four months till Kai was big enough and strong enough to start his actual training. By then, Mom and Gerry had gotten married at the farm, outside under a big striped awning near the fence. The guests included all our riders and horse owners, Dr. Small, Gerry's lawyer, who had become Mom's new best friend, and the horses watching from the meadow.

I was maid of honor in a light blue dress. I got to push Robbie, who was in a light blue suit. He carried a big blue pillow, with the wedding rings sewn onto it with a single strand of thread so they didn't roll off.

Mom wore a short white dress and a crown of white roses twined with cornflowers. I wore a similar crown. Robbie had a single rose and blue cornflower in his buttonhole, just like Gerry.

Kai stood near the fence in an actual shirt that Mom had made for him. It had puffy sleeves and a floppy collar, like something a medieval swordsman would have worn. He had a garland of flowers around his neck, matching Mom's crown. As the minister spoke, Kai translated his words into Horse for the herd in a wonderful cascade of whinnies and snorts.

Martha—who actually owned a blue dress and sandals—gave away the bride, saying, "But I'm not giving her away too far!"

At the end, when Gerry and Mom kissed, Bor bugled and reared up on his hind legs. Agora made a sound that was very much like a chuckle before racing along the fence in an ecstasy of emotion.

"Cool!" Joey Angotti said.

Even Angela Angotti smiled, which must have been a first.

Mr. Angotti was there with his wife. He was not at all what I'd imagined, being tall and handsome with very white teeth, hair long enough to braid, and a gold hoop in one ear.

The Proper kids applauded wildly.

Professor Harries wiped a tear away. I guessed she thought no one had seen her cry.

The newspaper reporters and photographers and the UPI guy and even the awful, weaselly Mr. Fern were there, too, all standing farther back, kept in place by several town cops. Mom and Gerry had given them permission under the advice of Adam Harding, the New York publicity man we'd hired to work on the newspaper and television coverage of anything to do with Kai and the plan to start up Kai's Kids.

Mr. Harding was nothing like my father's old publicist, whom Martha once described as "slick as snot." Instead, Harding was a quiet-spoken man who looked like a teacher or a librarian. He didn't argue a bit when Mom and Gerry made it clear that, apart from running expenses, all profits were to support the Kai's Kids Academy. Which made it a charitable foundation, an organization that raises money to support a good cause.

By this time, Kai (the human part) was as large and as smart as a teenager, and he loved speaking in public. He gave a big interview, talking with ease in front of the cameras. It turned out the rest of us were tongue-tied and shy in a studio and worse in front of a live audience. In fact, Gerry had twice threatened to pass out if we made *him* go on either radio or TV. And no one wanted Martha to say anything on TV in case it was something too sharp to help the cause.

The following month, Mr. Harding got Kai a huge photo shoot for *Life* magazine with Robbie—dressed like a cowboy—in his wheelchair by Kai's side.

Mr. Harding also helped us get smaller articles in *This Week Magazine*, a story and then later follow-ups in *Reader's Digest*, a spot on the *Steve Allen Show*, and a special appearance by Kai on *Captain Kangaroo*.

"*Captain Kangaroo!*" Robbie crowed. "That was my favorite show when I was little."

"You still watch it," I reminded him. "And you're not so big now."

☆ ☆ ☆

While Mr. Harding's publicity plan unfolded, Kai was learning how to carry children safely on his back. We started by using some of my dolls. I had two large ones that Mom called my "sleepers" because they shared the bed with me. Each one was the size of a three-year-old. Wolf Dad had bought them in New York when he'd played a major concert in the city, back when we were a family. Now they were Kai's.

I liked the idea that Kai was using the dolls given to me by Wolf Dad. At almost fourteen, I was well into irony.

We tied the dolls to a saddle on Kai's back. I walked on his right side, Martha on his left. Kai wore a set of leather straps, like a baby's halter, around his chest and over his shoulders. These were the reins that a handicapped child could hold on to, giving some feeling of control. Martha and I, walking by Kai's side, said things like *slow down, turn left carefully, back up*. In reality, Kai didn't need us there.

But after a day's work with us, Kai would take off into the field to run. He was still very much part horse and needed to "get out the kicks." We'd pulled down his fenced-in run when Mr. Harding said it gave the impression we were trying to hide something, not let the world in on the wonderful story of Kai.

The hardest part of our whole training was making sure Kai wore a shirt. Horses can stand a higher temperature than humans can. Their body temperature runs regularly between 99.5 and 101.4 degrees. And young horses run even higher. In that area, too, Kai was completely horse.

But as Mom told him, "It's more about being polite and professional. The parents will want you to have a shirt on before they'll allow a child to get that close to you."

More pointedly, Martha said, "No one wants a naked boy around their kid."

Kai smiled, that slow smile that always won us over. "Can I wear a T-shirt?"

Martha and Mom nodded.

So we went to a print shop and had several kinds made up. One said I'M NOT HORSING AROUND and had a picture of a pony on it. Two others said I LOVE HORSES. And one even had a centaur with a child on his back, with this line underneath: I'M ONE OF KAI'S KIDS.

I tried to convince Mom to get extras to sell to the riders. "They'll all want one."

She shook her head. "What happened to protecting Kai and not exploiting him?"

"I'm trying to make lemonade here, Mom."

"You're trying to make *money*."

I stared at her. "Well, of course, that too. It's all for the foundation." And then, realizing I was sounding just like my father, Wolf Dad, I threw my arms around her. "Sorry, sorry, sorry."

"It's a thin line, sweetie," she said, "between making lemonade and running a lemonade factory." She paused. "But as we seem to be starting a factory, we need to be sure it's an honest one. Mr. Harding is helping us do just that."

We ended up with a policy, suggested by Mr. Harding, that every child who rode in Kai's Kids Academy got a free

T-shirt. But if they wanted more, they would have to buy them. It had taken us about twenty seconds in a family meeting to come to full consensus on that one. Even Martha had nothing bad to say about the idea.

☆ ☆ ☆

By the end of the year, Kai's first rides had been thoroughly documented by a company in a full-length documentary that was nominated for an Oscar, though it didn't win. Robbie and a few local handicapped kids starred in it. The money we got for that quadrupled what we already had in the foundation account.

Gerry and Mom, with Mr. Angotti's help (turned out he's a builder), made Kai a much larger stall that stood next to Martha's house, with a front entrance for guests and a back entrance into the paddock and a covered breezeway that ran between his stall and Martha's kitchen. He had a floor-to-ceiling bookcase, a dresser filled with T-shirts, a small closet with room for more than the one jacket he owned, a phone jack and phone, a writing table with plenty of pens and paper and paints, a bigger refrigerator, a TV stand with a full-sized color TV, and shelves for all his board games.

Thirty handicapped children come regularly at least twice a month to ride Kai. And we're training other therapy horses as well, though none of them seem to be as popular as Kai.

Wolf Dad has written two or three times demanding a share of the foundation's profits, each time using a different lawyer. But Mom got a legal injunction against him, and he didn't demand money again. The mere threat of exposing what he called Robbie and Kai seemed to have scared him off.

☆ ☆ ☆

Have things always gone smoothly for us?

Nothing at a horse farm always goes smoothly. But it is working—better than I'd hoped for and much, much better than any of us ever expected.

AUGUST 1966

A New Shower of Stars

AND SO WE COME AROUND TO SUMMER AGAIN, *a full year since Kai was born. He looks, speaks, and acts as if he is all grown up, but he's never quite lost his sense of play, loving to kick up his heels in the meadow. He's not as tall as Gorn or Bor, but is quite a few hands higher than Agora and can now carry children up to the age of thirteen or fourteen, as long as they aren't terribly heavy.*

Our family went out to watch the Perseid shower.

Kai carried Robbie on his back, with Martha walking alone on one side just in case either one of them panicked in the night.

I'd packed a picnic basket filled with oat cookies and juices for Kai, sugar cookies and milk for Robbie and me, and a thermos of chamomile tea for the grown-ups, plus napkins and cups for us all.

Gerry and Mom hauled the blankets. Once in the paddock,

the blankets all laid out, Gerry got Robbie down and settled him on the blue blanket. Then he and Mom collapsed on the red. Martha kept standing next to Kai, as if she expected something bad to happen. Agora trotted around us once, then went over closer to the barn to graze.

Meanwhile, I spread out the old army blanket slightly away from the others, then lay down on my back. It took a minute for my eyes to adjust and then I could make out the stars shooting across the sky.

"Look!" I called out.

"Look! Look!" Robbie echoed and pointed.

Then Kai chimed in. "I see them!"

Mom and Gerry laughed at the sight of all those stars. Martha just rolled her eyes, but I think she was pleased.

I recalled that night two years earlier when something white and glowing had sailed over the fence between the Suss farm and ours, something I'd thought was a shooting star or ball of lightning.

I hadn't known it then, but it had been the beginning of the magic that I'd longed for. A different kind of magic than I'd expected. It had brought us Kai and a dad. It had brought my mother laughter and happiness.

So this time when a huge ball of light leaped the fence, I was prepared. But not prepared enough. This time the ball of light carried with it a large and glowing centaur in its center, who stepped sedately out through the light as if through a door.

He trotted up to the six of us, then stood still, hands on his waist as if waiting for an introduction. I could see he was very old. There were threads of white in his long mane, and his face was full of lines.

Kai moved toward him, stopped about two feet away, and made a half bow.

The old centaur greeted him with a series of whinnies, and Kai at first nodded, then shook his head.

"Speak the human tongue," Kai told him, "for this is my family, and only one of them speaks Horse."

"I will try, my son, but this is not my language. And I am not comfortable with its words," he said a bit stiltedly.

Turning to us, the old centaur continued. "First, I bring greetings to my son and then to all who have helped him in this year. He looks well cared for."

"He is well cared for," Martha grumbled. "No thanks to you."

The old centaur nodded at her politely as if she'd said something nice. "I am Chiron, and I have told my son it is time for him to come home."

Robbie pushed himself into a sitting position. "Kai is home, Mr. Chiron. Here. With us."

Chiron turned and addressed Robbie. "Your Kai does not belong here, human child. He has a duty—"

I jumped to my feet. "He has more than a duty here. He has a . . . a family. He has a calling. He has love."

Chiron wrinkled his nose at me. Perhaps he was thinking hard, perhaps he was smelling something bad. At that moment, I couldn't tell.

"We, his people, have great need of him. It is why he was made."

I couldn't help myself. Speaking almost without thought, but with a great deal of passion, I said, "Whatever he was made for, he is his own person now. He can make his own choices here. He chooses to work with children who aren't perfectly abled, and helps them gain power and a sense of their true worth."

That may have sounded like a quote from one of the articles about Kai, and in fact I'd said it first to a reporter.

"Ahhh." Smiling, Chiron raised a huge hand. "You are a young Diana. Well said, well challenged. I felt the arrow here." He held his hand over his heart as if mocking me. Or as if speaking like an alien on The Twilight Zone, which Mom and I used to watch.

Kai's shoulders went back as he steeled himself for some sort *of confrontation.* "Father Chiron, Wise One, Teacher of Princes, let me introduce you to my family. The girl you call Diana is my sister, Arianne, and she's as smart as she is beautiful."

Me, beautiful?

"My brother, Robbie, the heart of the family."

The centaur nodded. "I see the resemblance," *he said,* "for he is a dolphin child. You have the same eyes."

"My father-of-the-heart, Gerry. He's a doctor who heals animals."

"Ahhh, Hippocrates." Chiron nodded once more.

"And my three mothers—Mom."

Mom stood and made a sort of curtsy.

"Marmar." Martha held her hand up in the peace sign. I didn't even know she ever watched the news.

From the meadow, Agora whinnied, a series of rapid notes that sounded like a challenge.

"That's Mama," said Kai.

"Aha," Chiron said, and answered her in Horse, his voice low, as if he was sweet-talking her.

Martha had already started toward Agora. "I'll get her," *she called over her shoulder,* "but don't expect her to be glad to see you." *And then she was gone into the dark.*

When she returned with Agora, the pony stood anxiously

to one side, refusing to look at Chiron and shifting from one forefoot to the other.

"I don't want to leave these people, this family," Kai said simply.

Mom stepped forward. "He's still really just a boy, Chiron, too young to be taken away."

"Gracious mother," Chiron said, bowing his head to her, "the centaurs were created to be immortal. Death can come to us only through accident or murder. But we were also a quarrelsome and unruly folk and brought about our own destruction. I am the only one left, allowed by the Powers to come down to your world and help bring into being a new line of centaurs. I saw you and your family and the pony when I emerged from the light and knew at once you were good folk. I entrusted you with my only son for the year of his gestation and the year of his learning. But now—"

"You can't just take him!" Robbie cried. "He needs us. We need him. We . . . we love him."

Chiron pursed his lips. "I have always been puzzled by how much humans rely on love, when truth and honor are much better allies."

I stepped forward. "Will you make a bargain with us, great Chiron?"

He laughed. It was almost a horse snicker. "A bargain?"

"Leave Kai here for another year of learning. So he can help train others to take his place. He speaks both our language and Horse. And after, let him come back for visits . . . every solstice, and Christmas and . . ." I thought quickly. "July Fourth and my birthday and Robbie's."

Chiron stood thinking about that for a minute, then, turning to Kai, said, "What do you say, my son? I will not force you. To force someone to do what is right is itself wrong."

Kai went up to the old centaur and embraced him, then stepped back. "Old one, your reputation for wisdom has not been overstated. In a year, the school of horse therapy will be well established. I'd be honored to go with you and help bring back the centaur folk to the land of our grandfathers. But now my home, my family, my work—all I love—is here. I say love *because it is the finest of human emotions. It would be dishonorable to leave my loved ones right now. And I would think ill of you if you forced me to."*

Chiron thought for a long moment. "That is a bargain I can keep," he said. "And"—he looked right at me, his dark, wise eyes full of humor—"it is a rare human who can outbargain a Greek god."

"They say Quakers are great at making bargains," I said.

"What are Quakers?"

"You will have years to discover this," said Gerry with a chuckle.

We shook hands all around, except for Martha, to whom Chiron flashed the peace sign. She blushed.

Kai then showed his centaur father how Robbie could ride on his back, looking strong and whole, the shooting stars over their heads.

I gasped. It was the exact picture from my dream. Maybe that *had* been the real magic.

The old centaur nodded, as if only at that moment had he truly understood Kai's role in our world.

So we had food and drink and more laughter until—like any star in the sky—Chiron faded into the dawn.

I wasn't fooled into thinking he was a dream or that he was gone for good. Still, I knew he was an honorable god and would keep his side of the bargain.

Just as he knew we would keep ours. I would make sure of it. For all of us, but especially for my liminal brothers, Robbie and Kai.

ABOUT CENTAUR NAMES

Centaurs are creatures found in Greek mythology, and in Greek their names are pronounced a bit differently than you might think.

As a group the centaurs, or Kentauroi (KEN-tawr-oy), were savages—half man, half beast—who lived in the inhospitable mountains and forests of Greece. They were thought to be untrainable and untamable beings who often got drunk and acted in horrible ways: kidnapping women, killing men, stealing from their neighbors, quarreling with their friends. Eventually they became feared guardians of the gates of Hades (the Greek version of the Afterlife).

The one centaur who everyone agreed was entirely good was Chiron (KAI-ren; also spelled Cheiron or Kheiron), whose foster father was the god Apollo. Chiron was civilized and kind, with great knowledge and skill in medicine. Some of the princes he taught were Jason, Perseus, Ajax, and Theseus, among others.

Other centaurs of note were Pholus (FOE-lus), Nessus (NESS-us), and Centaurus (ken-TAWR-us).

AUTHOR'S NOTE

This book is a fantasy, but two things are not.

The first is the phenomenon of the thalidomide babies, commonly called seal children, which happened in the late 1950s and early 1960s, when doctors in Europe gave out thalidomide pills to pregnant women suffering from terrible morning sickness.

No one understood at the time that those pills would have hideous side effects, producing children with severe handicaps. In fact, doctors then believed that no drugs taken by a pregnant woman could cross the "placental barrier" and hurt a growing fetus. But the thalidomide effects soon became an international scandal as upward of 20,000 babies in forty-six countries were born with deformities ranging from flipperlike arms and legs to twisted hands with fused fingers or no thumbs to children being born with no limbs at all.

By 1961, the drug had been banned by most countries for use by pregnant women, but it was still sold in Canada until 1962.

My husband and I were spending a year traveling in Europe in 1965 when I found out I was pregnant. I was so terrified by the thalidomide scandal that I refused all medication, returning home severely iron deficient, something that was quickly rectified by taking iron tablets in my last trimester.

⭐ ⭐ ⭐

The second thing that's true is horse therapy, also called Riding for the Handicapped, Equine Assisted Therapy, and other similar titles. It is important to note that the word *disabled* didn't replace the word *handicapped* until the 1980s and 1990s, so I have used it throughout the story.

We cannot say exactly when horses were first trained to help those who were mentally or physically handicapped/disabled; however, we do know that in ancient Lydia in 600 B.C. it was recorded that people with various disabilities rode horses.

The first actual study of therapy riding was done in France in 1875 by Dr. Cassaign (or Chassaignac), who used riding to treat certain neurological disorders. In the 1920s in England, soldiers wounded in World War I were given riding therapy.

Lis Hartel was Danish dressage champion in 1943 and 1944 when she was struck by polio. The doctors thought she would never be able to walk again or ride, but she was determined to compete and practiced hard. She needed help getting on and off her horse, and had to walk with two canes, but still she won a silver medal for Denmark in dressage in the Helsinki Olympics in 1952 and again in the 1956 Melbourne games. And she dedicated herself from then on to helping handicapped riders.

In the 1950s, British physiotherapists were exploring ways to help people who suffered from many different kinds of disabilities and hit again upon the idea of using horses for therapy.

The English Riding for the Disabled Association (RDA) and the North American Riding for the Handicapped Association (NARHA) were both founded in the same year, 1969. After that, riding for the disabled got a huge boost, and it eventually became an accepted therapy around the world.

Horse therapy has strict rules about the kinds of horses to be used, their training, and safety measures for riders. It is as real as other therapies. Perhaps—as Ari and Robbie and Kai might say—"realer."